Murder on the Road Less Traveled

Robert W. Gregg

Published by FastPencil Publishing

Murder on the Road Less Traveled

First Edition

Print edition ISBN: 9781499904505

Copyright © Robert W. Gregg 2018

http://www.fastpencil.com

Printed in the United States of America

❧

I owe a debt of gratitude to many people, but particularly to Kurt Foster, who helped me navigate the transition to a new computer, and Lois Gregg, who edited the text which became Murder on the Road Less Traveled.

PROLOGUE

The calendar said it was June 5th, and a warm late spring breeze was stirring the trees and the flags in and around Southport's town square. It was only 8 am, but the square was crowded. The reason for the crowd was readily apparent: there were nearly as many bicycles on the grass and walkways as there were people, and a majority of those people were wearing helmets and colorful short sleeve jerseys. This was the day when Crooked Lake was staging its annual Gravel Grinder, a fact that was spelled out for those who had just happened on the event by a large red and yellow banner that flapped in the breeze above Market Street.

It is doubtful that anyone in the crowd was a savant, able quickly and accurately to identify the number of bikes and riders in the square. But Joe Reiger, who had organized the event and kept a record of those who would participate and had contributed to its fund for charity, knew that the number was close to 155. There would be a few latecomers, of course, not to mention the occasional cancellation. But these were bikers, and bikers take their sport seriously, even when what they are embarking on is not a race with a winner. Virtually everyone who had signed up would be present when the Gravel Grinder started.

As was to be expected, many of the bikers knew each other. They had done this before, in some cases many times. Some donned their biking gear daily, often before breakfast, because it was a habit, and a good one at that. Now, as the starting time approached, they were chatting good naturedly, checking their equipment, stocking up on some last minute refreshment for the road and what would be a ride that could well last for close to five hours. One of the riders was Ernie Eakins, a 32 year old veteran of these events. He had already logged nearly four miles, having biked down from his home on the hill northwest of Southport. His wife, Connie, who was a much more casual biker, had offered to drive him to the town square.

"No point in wearing yourself out before the race," she had said.

"No problem. It'll just be a short warm-up, mostly downhill. What's more, it isn't a race. So I'll meet you at the finish line. Why don't you aim for one o'clock? There'll be burgers and coffee; then you can take me home."

Little did Connie know that Ernie wouldn't be at the finish line at one o'clock. Or at two. Or for that matter when dusk descended on Crooked Lake that evening.

CHAPTER 1

The crowd that had filled Southport's town square at the beginning of the Gravel Grinder had largely dissipated by 9 am, but it was fast reassembling by the time the clock on the Methodist church tower struck one. Several of the bikers had already completed the course, and were standing around the cooking wagon which had been set up on the square. Others could be seen turning onto Market Street and heading toward the finish line. As usual, some participants had treated the event as if it were a race, or something close to one; not surprisingly, they were among the first to return to the square. Others, a clear majority of those who had signed up for the Gravel Grinder, knew that they were in for a long and demanding morning and felt no need to push themselves to the limit. They would be returning to the square sometime in the next hour, satisfied that they had done what they had set out to do and made their contribution to a worthwhile cause.

Joe Reiger was aware that two of those who had committed to the event had had to withdraw at the last minute, Bill Donovan because his wife had gone into labor and Jenny Flowers because she had awakened with a temperature of 102. Otherwise everyone who had made a commitment had been a part of the closely packed group of cyclists who had left Southport shortly after eight. There would be a few laggards, of course, but eventually all of the rest would cross the finish line and hit the food line (Joe always made sure that there was enough even for those for whom cycling a fair distance was a more challenging task than they had imagined it would be).

Cycling, at least for many of those who participated in the season's Gravel Grinder, was a community sport, a shared form of exercise, a satisfying opportunity to renew acquaintances. Evidence of this social value of biking was omnipresent in Southport's town square that afternoon. Rather than head immediately for home, many of the men and women who had just completed roughly 150 miles of cycling found themselves engaged in swapping stories about a particularly rough road, a spectacular view from a hilltop, the occasionally inconsiderate driver, or minor problems that needed fixing and sometimes gave vent to expletives.

Gradually these post-ride conversations petered out and the cyclists and their friends and families went home. One person who didn't was Connie Eakins. She had expected Ernie by one, or no later than 1:15. After all, he rode, often considerable distances, several times every week, and he prided himself on being in good shape. There would be no trouble spotting him, even in the crowd that would be gathering on the square, or so she had told herself. He always wore a distinctive blue and yellow helmet and stood a ramrod 6' 5" tall. Unfortunately, she had not spotted him by 1:15. At 1:30 she began making the rounds of the bikers, inquiring as to whether anyone had seen him somewhere on the course. Few had and most of those remembered their encounters as having taken place in the early going on the road toward Watkins. It was not until little more than a corporal's guard was left in the square that she ran into Lou Coughlin as he was saying good-bye to Reiger.

"Hi, Lou. I'm beginning to worry about Ernie. He should have been back an hour ago. You see him anywhere along the way?"

"Hi, Connie. Long time, no see. Sorry, but I don't remember seeing Ernie since we took that cut-off above Waneta. I wouldn't worry. He probably had one of those pesky problems with a tire. Happens all the time. Didn't he call?"

"That's what's bothering me. He had his cell with him, always does. Promised to stay in touch. But no call. And he always carries a spare, so I can't imagine him stuck somewhere on the course with a bike that won't perform."

"Sounds right. Not sure which of his bikes he was riding, but he's got several good ones and he's a bear about maintenance. My guess is that he stopped off somewhere to see a friend, just forgot to tell you. Why don't you call around, give him hell that he stranded you down here on the square?"

"Thanks," Connie said, making no effort to hide her worry. "You know him better than that. Just about every cyclist we know around the lake was in this race or whatever it is, so I doubt that he stopped to say hello to anybody."

"Maybe he had a collision with some crazy, irresponsible driver," Reiger interrupted. "How about checking the hospital over in Yates Center?"

This wasn't the kind of advice Connie wanted to hear.

"My husband's an excellent driver, whether in his car or on one of his bikes. He's never had an accident, or, to the best of my memory, even a close call."

"I'm sure you're right, but accidents do happen." Joe shared Mrs. Eakins' worry, but he was also anxious to wrap up the Gravel Grinder. "Look, maybe Ernie just decided to go directly home, spare you the need to pick him up down here in Southport."

"No, we agreed I'd drive him home. Besides, the race would have been over hours ago. If he went straight home, don't you suppose he'd have thought it strange I wasn't there?"

Neither Joe nor Lou believed that there wasn't some perfectly innocent explanation for Ernie Eakins' failure to meet up with his wife at the end of the day's big event. But the town square was now largely empty, and Lou, who was anxious to head home, had one more idea.

"If you're really worried, maybe you should call the sheriff."

"Call the sheriff?" It was clear that Connie found the suggestion frightening. The only reason for calling the sheriff would be that she feared something terrible had happened to her husband.

"That's what I would do," Joe said. "No point making a 411 call. I've got the number at my desk. Come on over to my office and we'll let the sheriff's office know that Ernie is missing."

Connie proceeded to sit down on the nearest bench.

"You really think the sheriff should know about this?"

"Just covering the bases," Joe said. "She'll be more likely to have an idea about him being missing than I do. Or Lou. Come on, let's do it."

"Oh, God. I was worried, and then I was getting mad at him. Now he may be dead. What do I -"

"No point in sitting here. Let's make that call." Joe thought that Connie was beginning to sound hysterical. He wrapped an arm around her shoulders and they started for the Chamber of Commerce building across the square.

"He's okay, I'm sure. Probably wondering about you." For the first time since Connie Eakins had told him that she and Ernie had missed connections at the end of the Gravel Grinder, Joe Reiger had a premonition that something was seriously wrong.

CHAPTER 2

The sheriff of Cumberland County was only mildly concerned about the annual Gravel Grinder. There were always a few complaints about cyclists clogging the roads, slowing down traffic. She always had to assign all of her officers to the narrow but more heavily travelled highways near the lake and in the local villages. But Kevin was not a biker, and Carol knew from experience that those who were would have had a good day and that a goodly sum would have been raised for whatever charity had been chosen as this year's beneficiary.

Having taken the few precautions that she regularly took for events like this, she had put it out of her mind and turned her attention to more serious matters. It was 4:38 when JoAnne appeared at her door with the news that Joe Reiger from the Southport Chamber of Commerce was on the line.

"What seems to be on his mind?" Carol asked. She hadn't seen or heard from Joe in close to a year.

"Something about one of the cyclists not getting back on time from today's race."

"I don't think they had a race. Just one of those affairs where all the guys who ride a bike around here have themselves a workout on our roads, including those that never get paved."

"I think it isn't just men who do it," JoAnne observed, a rare correction of her boss.

Too late Carol remembered that JoAnne was a serious cyclist.

"Sorry. I really do know better. But why do you suppose Reiger is calling me? It doesn't sound like a law and order issue."

"He didn't say, just that one of the bikers is missing."

"Okay. I'll see what he thinks we should do."

Carol got herself a cup of coffee and picked up he phone.

"Hello, Joe. You've had one of your big days, I'm sure. What's this about a missing biker?"

"I'm not sure I should be bothering you, sheriff, but Ernie Eakins - you know Ernie? - he was one of our participants today and he never checked in after it was over. His wife is here with me, and she's worried sick."

"Why don't you put her on the phone."

"I'd be careful if I were you. She's a nervous wreck."

"It can't be that bad. He's probably at some friend's place. Let me talk to her."

Carol waited for what seemed like two or three minutes. Carol tried to imagine what was going on down in Southport. Was the young woman refusing to talk with the sheriff? When she finally said hello, it was obvious that she had been reluctant to do so.

"You're the sheriff?"

"Yes I am. I understand that you want to talk about your husband. Mr. Reiger tells me that he was on the Lake's annual ride, but that he didn't meet you like you expected him to when it was over."

"That's true. Joe thought maybe you could help me."

"You understand that this is out of my line. I mean it doesn't sound like my job description. Isn't it more likely that you could find your husband by calling your friends - his friends? There must have been a lot of them with him on the ride today. He probably stopped off at one of their homes."

"But he was to meet me in the town square, and he didn't show up. He didn't call or anything. What am I going to do?"

"Like I said, I'd start calling friends. Or just go back home and wait for him. I'll bet he called and left a message for you."

"He could have called me on my cell. Besides, the ride ended a long time ago. Ernie's never done something like this. What if he got killed and couldn't call?"

Carol knew nothing about the relationship between the Eakins. What she did know was that the Gravel Grinder was an annual event, usually involving well over one hundred cyclists, and that no one had ever been injured, much less killed, on any of them. There had to be a simple explanation for today's situation. But she knew that she couldn't just give this woman, who was obviously panicked, her assurance that all would soon be well.

"Let's assume that your husband might have had a fall and needed some help. Not likely, but I suppose it's possible. Why don't you let me call the hospitals in this area and see if your husband, by any chance, has been brought in. I'm sure the answer will be no, but it'll put your mind at ease to know. You stay with Mr. Reiger - I'll call back within fifteen minutes. Try to relax."

"I'm scared to death. Ernie's in trouble, I know. I hope he's alive."

Connie Eakins didn't give the phone back to Joe Reiger. She hung up. The sheriff knew that she had been of no help to Mrs. Eakins, so she dutifully placed a few calls and quickly learned that her husband had not been admitted to any hospital. In all probability he was at that very minute enjoying a beer with a fellow biker somewhere in the vicinity of Crooked Lake, unaware that he had thoughtlessly alarmed his wife. Or that his worried wife knew less about the social pleasures of biking than her husband did.

CHAPTER 3

The pressure of business and common sense told Carol to put her conversation with Mrs. Eakins behind her. But for some reason she found herself reflecting for several long minutes on that conversation before turning to her in-basket. Surely the worried wife was making a mountain out of the proverbial mole hill. But was she? What if her husband's failure to meet her at the Gravel Grinder's finish line was such an aberration that it deserved more than a casual dismissal? What if one or more of Ernie Eakins' fellow riders had seen something or heard something on the course that merited a serious investigation?

Deputy Sheriff Bridges interrupted this preoccupation with the unlikely by calling to remind her that they had agreed to have a meeting about some trouble which seemed to be brewing in nearby Walkertown regarding an overzealous towing company. It appeared that she was five minutes late for the meeting.

It was with a sigh of relief that she told Sam she'd be with him in a few seconds. She wouldn't mention the Eakins' situation. If she hadn't put it out of her mind by the time she got back to the cottage at day's end, she'd ask Kevin what he thought. She was confident that he would tell her to forget about it. Unless, of course, he thought he smelled another Crooked Lake murder. That thought produced a smile. She grabbed a file and headed for Sam's office.

Kevin, much to her surprise, was busily typing away at his computer when she arrived home.

"What are you doing?" she asked.

"Writing my article on Brahms' operas," he replied.

"My memory's better than that. You've told me several times that Brahms never wrote an opera. So what are you doing?"

"Writing about why Brahms never wrote an opera. It may go nowhere, but I thought I'd give it a try."

"Why don't you give it a rest and pour some wine while I get out of this uniform. I think I have a non-starter that will make Brahms look like Verdi."

"Meaning you had a dull day," Kevin said as he hit the save key.

"I thought I'd let you decide that."

Ten minutes later they repaired to the deck and Carol gave Kevin a quick summary of the annual Gravel Grinder, including its confusing conclusion.

"What am I supposed to make of all that? I last rode a bicycle when I was a paper boy, and that was a lifetime ago. If it had been me who never got back to the town square, I'd chalk it up to the fact that anything more than a mile would have worn me out. I'd be asleep on the roadside at the outskirts of Southport."

"Oh, come on. You can swim a mile without working up a sweat. That's not the point. The question is whether Mrs. Eakins has reason to be anxious about what happened to her husband. I take it she didn't call here this afternoon. She didn't, did she?"

"No, nor did anyone else, about the Gravel Grinder or anything else. It's been a quiet day."

"That's what I figured. I won't learn anything new, but if you'll excuse me I'm going to give Mrs. Eakins a call. She'll either be a nervous wreck or she won't answer the phone. She'll be out, driving the county highways and byways, looking for her husband."

Two minutes later Carol resumed her seat on the deck.

"No answer, and I doubt that it's because Ernie finally arrived and they've gone out to dinner."

"Well, I'm afraid I haven't anything resembling a eureka moment," Kevin said. "But the *Gazette* reported that well over one hundred - I think it was 150 something - were going to participate in the Gravel Grinder. Which means that if something happened to Eakins along the way one or more of the other riders would surely have been aware of it and helped him or called for help. It would be pretty hard to disappear with that many fellow bikers on the course with you. But you've already told me that no one reported that he had had an accident. Ergo, the odds that he did have one would be pretty small."

"That's what it looks like to me," Carol agreed. "None of the area hospitals and emergency care centers admit to seeing Eakins. And none of the other cyclists have had anything to say about why he might be missing."

"But you're assuming that there were always other riders around Eakins. What if he broke away from the crowd, either going hell bent for election, leaving the others in his dust, or slowing down until the rest of the riders were out of sight ahead of him. Either way something could have happened to him that none of the other riders saw. Oh, and here's another possibility. What if Eakins and another rider had a bad relationship, were arguing as they rode along, and then got into a fight which left him dead on the roadside?"

Carol wasn't having it.

"That's absolutely crazy. Cyclists who participate in events like this are a pretty close knit group. The odds that a fellow rider despised Eakins and used a road race to kill him have to be less than nil. We're talking about Crooked Lake, for God's sake, not the Tour de France where an international reputation may be on the line. I have no intention of turning the Gravel Grinder into a murder case."

"I know, we've had enough murders up here to last for a generation. Maybe two. So I'm not making a case for another one. All I'm doing is suggesting that our many cyclists aren't necessarily part of the tight knit group you think they are. We don't know the great majority of riders who were on the course today. For all we know, Eakins was screwing another rider's wife or something equally heinous. If I were you, I'd start interviewing the lot of them, finding out who didn't like Eakins."

"The lot of them?" Carol asked. "One hundred fifty, maybe more? Good way to alienate the local population, don't you think? No thank you."

"You're almost certainly right, but you wanted my input - for what it's worth. So we leave it up to Mrs. Eakins, let her handle a routine case of misunderstanding. If you need more help, I'll be at my computer, doing myself some professional good."

"I'll keep that in mind."

CHAPTER 4

When the sheriff reached her office the next morning, she had resolved to leave the Eakins matter to the Eakins. She had fallen into the bad habit of letting issues like this deprive her of sleep. Ironically, her discussion of the matter with Kevin the previous evening had had the opposite effect. There was no persuasive reason to treat Ernie's disappearance as a matter of law and order. Although Kevin had suggested the possibility that Ernie was the victim of a fellow rider's hostility, she had not been persuaded that he was really serious. More likely that he had simply become addicted to the view that Crooked Lake was due for a murder every year. Well, she had decided before falling asleep, not this year.

The squad meeting went off without any reference to the Gravel Grinder. In all probability, she thought, her officers - or most of them - knew nothing about Ernie Eakins' failure to finish what she still thought of as the big race. In any event, it had not been a race, which made it even less likely that his disappearance was a matter of any great consequence. When Carol returned to her office, she was prepared to turn her attention to more prosaic questions.

"Hi, Carol." JoAnne was at her door. "You've already had a phone call. We ought to have a policy that tells the citizenry we don't answer the phone before ten unless it's an emergency."

"I take it that this isn't an emergency."

"It doesn't sound like one, but people have a way of thinking that a routine is a crisis."

"So I should call back," Carol said. "Okay, who is it?"

"Says her name is Connie Eakins," JoAnne said, unaware that she had just spoiled her boss's day.

Carol sighed, took the note with the number on it, and tried to adopt a positive attitude. The wayward husband had reappeared.

"Good morning, Mrs. Eakins. I hope you're calling with good news."

The voice on the other end of the line made it clear the minute her caller started speaking that the news was not good.

"It's bad news, worse than yesterday," Connie said. "Still no word from Ernie, nothing from Joe Reiger, nothing from anyone."

"You say the situation is worse than yesterday. What do you mean?"

"Just that I was sure - or tried to be - that somebody would tell me something that was promising. But no one called, and everyone I called was sorry for me but knew nothing that was helpful. Most everyone didn't even know Ernie wasn't home."

"I'm so sorry. I suppose I had expected that by this time your husband had returned or you'd have heard something from him."

"Nothing like this has ever happened to us. I'm beside myself, and I really need your help."

The sheriff had made up her mind only thirteen hours previously that the problem of Ernie Eakins' disappearance was not hers to solve. Now his wife was virtually demanding that she take responsibility for a problem she very much wanted nothing to do with.

"Have you been in touch with your husband's friends? His immediate family, or at least those he was closest to?" Carol doubted that the frantic woman on the phone line had done so. There hadn't been time to visit all of his friends; as for relatives, Carol had no idea who they were or how close they were.

"You said that you really need my help. How do you think I can be of any help?"

"I want you to find my husband's body. That's what sheriffs do, isn't it?"

"That means you think he's dead." Carol was surprised. Almost immediately she realized that she shouldn't be. "Why do you think he's dead? After all, there must be a lot of people you haven't contacted, people who could give you information about him."

"He's dead," Mrs. Eakins insisted. "If he were alive, he would have been in touch with me."

"But you can't be sure of that. He may have tried to reach you, explain where he was, what he was doing, but didn't get through."

"I know you want to reassure me, sheriff, but he's dead. You don't know Ernie. He would never, *ever*, go off somewhere without telling me. I don't know much about the course they were riding yesterday, but it was all right here in the Finger Lakes. You've got to take the route Ernie took and follow it, all the way from the Southport town square back to the finish line. I'd do it, but I'm not sure what I'd be looking for. But you, it's your profession. You'd see things that didn't look right. You could ask people what they saw, whether Ernie stopped off, you know, to ask questions or something. I can't bring him back but he needs a proper burial. Please help me."

Carol was in a corner. She could either be the sheriff and say 'no' or a good samaritan and say 'yes.' She knew what she had to do.

"I hope you're wrong about your husband, but I can see that you need help finding out what happened. I'll do what I can. Mr. Reiger will give me the details about the route the cyclists took yesterday; I may even be able to persuade him to accompany me. In any event, I'll check every square inch of the area of the ride and let you know what I find - or can't find."

"Oh, thank you, sheriff. I'd probably be kidding myself if I thought you would find Ernie, but I know you'll do your best."

Mrs. Eakins did sound grateful, although Carol found it hard to believe that her willingness to search for his body made her day.

CHAPTER 5

Carol had been surprised that Kevin had not kidded her about her willingness to help Connie Eakins.

"You're almost too nice to be a sheriff, do you know that?" he had said after hearing about his wife's response to the woman's appeal for assistance in finding her husband's body. "She needs help, and you came through for her."

"I couldn't say no," Carol agreed.

"That's what I mean."

The early part of the next morning was spent in Joe Reiger's office in the Chamber of Commerce. He had been more than willing to see her, and, as Carol quickly discovered, had much less on his plate than she did.

"You think you can find Eakins?" he asked.

"No, I don't. But the woman's having a breakdown, not that I blame her. At least I hope to discover what all the bikers were up to yesterday when they went on what you call the Gravel Grinder. What I need is a detailed map that shows where they went. I know most of the roads around here, but of course I don't have a good picture of every route they followed. I assume that Gravel Grinder means the riders didn't stay on paved roads. If you have a map left, perhaps you can let me have it. Or better yet, if you have the time, you could join me while I navigate the course they followed."

Carol thought that Joe would plead a busy schedule and wish her luck, but she was right in her assumption that he really had

time on his hands, if only he didn't pretend that he didn't. He
didn't.

"You'd get lost if you did what you propose to do on your own.
Too many side roads, confusing intersections, places where nobody has ever heard of paving. I'll go with you. Or better yet, unless
you think you have to be in an official car, I'll drive. Give you more
of a chance to look around, see what you're looking for."

"I'm not really looking for anything in particular. I certainly don't
expect to see Ernie Eakins' body lying in a roadside culvert. But if
you could go with me, I'd be very grateful. And I like the idea of you
doing the driving, if your schedule permits."

Joe Reiger's face lit up. In fact, Carol thought she saw his chest
grow temporarily larger. He's now part of an official investigation,
and he'll be pleased to tell people about it.

The trip itself turned out to be an eye opener, with beautiful
views of two lakes, woods that Carol had never visited, and hills
that were surprisingly steep. It was also, as Joe had suggested,
confusing. It began on what passed in this area for main roads,
easy to navigate. But once it had climbed a hill outside of Southport, it took the first of what would be half a dozen exits onto sec-
ondary roads. Tertiary might be a better term. Initially it looked as
if they were headed north, but it wasn't long before they were going east, then south, and, after awhile, in a direction that was hard
to figure out under a cloudy, sunless sky.

"Who creates these routes?" Carol asked.

"Depends on who you ask," Joe answered. "I'm technically in
charge, so I suppose you could say I pick the course. But over the
years quite a few people have had a say. The veteran cyclists, of
course. There'll be places where you're confronted with options,
like that place we passed through a couple of miles ago. They can
be kind of fun. Go one way and you're headed for a dead end, go
another and first thing you know you'll be facing another choice -
a one lane dirt road to the left, a pot holed stretch to the right. We
try to keep the riders on their toes."

Joe stopped, mid-thought. Perhaps it had occurred to him that Ernie Eakins had, at just such a location, not been on his toes.

"Sort of like Frost's 'The Road Not Taken,'" she said, only to realize seconds later that Reiger didn't know what she was talking about. Neither did she, on second thought. Without thinking about it, she'd been showing off.

"Do you have the impression that your riders do get lost from time to time?"

"No question, it's happened. Usually no problem. You discover that nothing looks right, so you turn around and retrace your steps. Or your wheels - you know what I mean."

"I've seen signs here and there. It looks like you try to keep everyone on the straight and narrow."

"We try to do that, but sign posts don't last. People are always taking them down, complaining that they will mislead drivers other than those in a race or some other bike outing. See that corner up ahead, where there's a switchback? No sign. I know there was one there yesterday."

Carol gradually realized that the Gravel Grinder had been a long one. Not only did it frequently take her into territory with which she was unfamiliar; it also seemed to back track now and then, and, with the exception of the small town of Grovespring, managed to avoid paved roads.

But her purpose had been to see if anywhere along the way there was anything - a roadside house or barn, a hidden gully or debris field - which just might have something to do with Ernie's disappearance.

"I've enjoyed the drive. Thanks for introducing me to no man's land in upstate New York. But frankly I haven't seen anything that's likely to encourage Mrs. Eakins. You haven't seen anything that looks unusual, have you?"

"No, but my assignment has to do with chauffeuring you around the county. I've always assumed that Ernie used the occasion to visit friends or relatives, but I don't know the Eakins well enough to make that more than a guess. You aren't really looking for his body, are you?"

"Yes and no. But between us, and please don't discuss this with anyone else, Ernie's wife is inclined to dismiss every ordinary explanation for his failure to make it home. Which has her worried that he's dead. I hope to disabuse her of that view, which is why we've been doing what we're doing today. So far I've seen nothing that gives me a clue that he's either alive or dead, but I didn't expect to. So back to my question about you seeing anything unusual. Forget about how things look - I'm sure they look like they do day in and day out. But what about side roads, roads that weren't on the map the cyclists were following. You said that it was easy to get lost, make a wrong turn. Have we passed any side road that Ernie could have taken by mistake? I'm not suggesting anything, just trying to consider every possibility."

"Oh, lord, that's a tough one. We've probably passed three dozen or more dirt driveways to old trailers or barely habitable shacks. I can't imagine why Ernie or anyone else would take one of those God forsaken roads. It's pretty obvious that they aren't a way to any place except somebody's ramshackle home. Or an abandoned house that never got torn down. There are a lot of them around here, but you know that as well as I do."

"I'm afraid so," Carol said. Like Joe, she couldn't imagine why Ernie would have taken any of these side roads to nowhere.

It had been a long and tiring morning when they got back to Southport. Carol knew nothing about Ernie Eakins that she hadn't known before the drive. She knew a great deal more about what a Gravel Grinder was, including the fact that she was happy that she got her exercise in other less exhausting ways.

CHAPTER 6

The next morning Carol was engaged in uncharacteristic procrastination, doing whatever she could to avoid the call she had to make to Connie Eakins. She had promised herself that she would do it at ten o'clock; but it was already 10:25, and she was stalling by handling some correspondence which was conspicuously non-urgent.

JoAnne interrupted this piece of routine business to report that a couple of people named Kennedy were sitting in the outer office and that they hoped to see her 'if it wasn't too much trouble.'

"They're very concerned that they may be bothering you, and would be glad to come back at another time. I said I'd see."

"They say what's on their mind?"

"Only that it concerns their son."

"Why don't you give me five more minutes and then bring them in. Kennedy, you say."

"Right. Ruth and Henry Kennedy. They're African-American."

Carol urged them to have the two seats across from her and offered them coffee, which they politely accepted - 'cream and sugar, please.'

"I don't believe we've met," she said. It was apparent that they were ill at ease, and she tried to encourage them to relax. "I'm Carol Kelleher, and I'm the sheriff of Cumberland County, as you must know. It's Mr. and Mrs. Kennedy, according to my assistant. What brings you here today?"

"It's a complicated story," Mr. Kennedy said. "We shouldn't be taking much of your time, but -"

"Let me tell her, Henry." Mrs. Kennedy spoke up. "He's right, it is complicated. But the real problem is quite simple. Our son is missing. The man he's working for called us yesterday and told us he'd disappeared. We're new here and we don't know many people. That includes Adolph Slocomb. He's the man Martin is helping."

"It probably wasn't a very good idea to agree to let him work out there," Mr. Kennedy interrupted. "We'd didn't really know Mr. Slocomb. But he needed help and we were anxious to find a place where Martin could get away from the house and get some fresh air. Anyway, now he's run away. At least Mr. Slocomb doesn't know where he is."

A second man gone missing in only two days. And the Kennedys were obviously not sure how to go about the task of telling their story. They seemed to be right, Carol thought. It is going to be complicated.

"Excuse me," Carol said. "Let's go back to the beginning. Your son is missing and he has been working for a Mr. Slocomb. Why don't you tell me something about your son and about Mr. Slocomb."

The Kennedys looked at each other, as if trying to decide who should answer the sheriff. As she had expected, Mrs. Kennedy finally decided that it was her responsibility.

"Our son is Martin Luther Kennedy. He's only fourteen years old, and he needs help. That's why we moved to Southport. But that's another story. Anyway, we advertised in the local paper to see if someone needed handyman kind of help this summer. There weren't many responses. Most people wanted someone older, more experienced. But Mr. Slocomb was interested. He came to our house and talked to us. And to Martin. As it turned out, he agreed to take our son on, even was willing to pick him up in the morning and bring him back in the evening. The pay wasn't very good, but after all Martin had no experience. So we agreed, and we thought everything was going well until yesterday when Slocomb called to tell us that Martin had disappeared. I called this morning, and Slocomb said he never came back or left a note explaining what he was doing. Of course he couldn't have written a note. Now he's gone, heaven knows where, and he won't be able to find his way home."

Mrs. Kennedy's report had said little about the son's disappearance, but it had said a great deal about the son.

For one thing, the boy is not only young. He needs help. What does that mean? That he's sick? But it sounded worse than that. No note to Mr. Slocomb because he couldn't have written one? For a fleeting moment Carol imagined that the boy had injured his hands, or had had a serious accident and lost their use. But no, a handicap like that would make him an impossible choice as Slocomb's handyman. Perhaps he's mentally retarded? And the business about being unable to find his way home. Certainly a fourteen year old would have no difficulty doing that, not in an area where Crooked Lake offered so many benchmarks.

"Forgive me, but I'm confused," Carol said. "You say that Martin needs help. I don't wish to pry, but if I'm going to help you find your son I suspect I'm going to have to know more about him and why he needs help."

Mrs. Kennedy looked down at her lap and Carol had the distinct impression that she was holding back tears.

"Martin is not what you'd call normal," she said. It was now clear that she *was* crying.

"Take your time, Mrs. Kennedy. This is obviously a difficult subject, hard to talk about. I have lots of time."

"Thank you. Martin has never been a typical kid, not since I brought him home from the hospital. But Henry and I didn't begin to know how difficult it would be to raise him. His situation became progressively worse. The doctors - there were lots of them - tried to help, and in a way they did, I suppose. At least they diagnosed his problem, although neither Henry nor I really understand all of it. It's a genetic problem, which means, I'm afraid, that he could have inherited it from us. Martin had down's syndrome at birth. I'm sure you know what that's like. Kids look different. You know they will never be able to function quite like other kids. But Martin also turned out to have something the doctors called ASD. Correct me if I'm wrong, Henry, but I think that stands for autism spectrum disorder. The two problems together can be severe and, unfortunately, Martin is a serious case. The truth is that we really haven't known how to raise him, but he's our boy and God in his wisdom has made him our responsibility."

Henry Kennedy, still dry eyed, took over the conversation.

"There's nothing you can do about Martin's mental or physical condition, sheriff, but maybe you can help us find him. You probably think it's a bit strange that we live in Southport. We don't know how many African-American families live around here, but we know there aren't many. I'm sure they came to this part of the country for different reasons, and we hope they're glad they did. In our case, we settled here, a long way from our old home in Charlotte, to protect Martin. He was treated cruelly down there, taunted all the time because he was different. School was an awful ordeal for him. He didn't know how to handle it. I'm not sure he really understood why he was treated like he was. Finally, Ruth and I figured we had to do something. I'm not sure why we picked a small town like the one up here."

"Yes, we do know, Henry," Ruth said. "We thought it would get us away from the kids that made his life hell. Sorry, I shouldn't be using words like that. Anyway, we had the good fortune of meeting the Hacketts on that visit last fall."

"The Hacketts?" Carol asked. "I believe I know a Rachel Hackett."

"That's the one. We met her at the school. She said they'd found the town of Southport - and the school - friendly. Well, maybe not exactly friendly, but live and let live. We've had no problems with neighbors and the school has worked hard to help Martin. The school counselor who really made our move possible is Francine Chartrell. She'd be glad to talk with you, I'm sure. But she can't find Martin. That's what we hope you can do."

"If I'm to help, perhaps you can tell me a bit more abut him. Of course I'll be talking to Mr. Slocomb, but you know your son better. How does he cope with his problems? I guess I'm asking whether he's inclined to go wandering off, or does he normally stay around the house, close to you. I'm including Mr. Slocomb and his place. Did he talk much with you about what he does when he goes to work?"

"Frankly, he doesn't talk much at all, and he's hardly said anything about Mr. Slocomb and what his days up on the hill are like."

"How long has he been with Mr. Slocomb?"

"Not long. Less than two weeks."

"Has Mr. Slocomb talked with you about how things are working out?"

"We wish we had asked more questions," Henry said. "We were always glad when he dropped Martin off, but we didn't want to sound too much like - what is the expression they're using today, helicopter parents? I suppose we worried that Mr. Slocomb might change his mind if we seemed to be second guessing him."

Second guessing him? Asking questions about how a severely handicapped son was doing in a new relationship with a man he didn't know? With a man that they couldn't have known well either? Carol couldn't imagine why the Kennedys were so reluctant to discuss their son with Slocomb. In the circumstances, to do so would have been both natural and wise. The more she heard about the arrangement they had struck with the man who needed a handyman, the more she found herself puzzling about that arrangement.

"Did you ever visit Mr. Slocomb's home, the place where Martin was working?"

"I'm afraid not," Ruth said, sounding guilty. "We should have, shouldn't we? You'll think we're bad parents, just glad to have days when we could lead a normal life, without constant reminders of our sad problem."

Yes, Carol thought, you should have. If it had been Kevin and me, we would certainly have been more involved in Martin's daily life. But we have never walked in the Kennedys' shoes. Now she was the one who was feeling guilty.

She chose to gather more information which could be useful by changing the subject.

"I hope you won't mind a few more questions. Personal questions. What is it that you do here in Southport, beside taking care of Martin, which must be pretty much a full time job?"

Her question sought answers from both of them, but it was Henry who spoke up first.

"It's a temporary appointment while I shop for something more challenging, but I work at Jefferson's Hardware in Yates Center. I've been thinking -"

"Henry was the assistant manager of a computer service outlet in Charlotte," Ruth interrupted, anxious to make the point that her husband moved in more prestigious commercial circles before moving to Southport.

"Sounds interesting, and I hope your plan for a more challenging position here works out for you," Carol said, addressing Mr. Kennedy. "As for you, Mrs. Kennedy, I assume that of necessity you have the major responsibility for Martin."

"That's been true, but with Martin up at Mr. Slocomb's during the week I've been working - well, volunteering is more like it - at the Southport library. It's been a part time job since last winter, and I would like it to be permanent. Of course, everything depends on Martin." She didn't have to say that it depended on whether he could be found. Nor did she sound as if she were optimistic that a full time appointment was in the cards even if he returned to the family nest.

It wasn't a promising situation, although it sounded as if both Kennedys possessed the skills necessary for good employment, at least by Crooked Lake standards. The more important issue at the moment was Martin's whereabouts, and Carol realized that she felt very differently about it than she did the disappearance of Ernie Eakins. She had reluctantly assumed responsibility for finding Eakins, but Martin Kennedy was an altogether different story. Unlike Eakins, Martin was young, mentally disturbed, and unable to care for himself. It was not primarily as sheriff that she knew she must help the Kennedys. It was a moral obligation.

"I am really sorry that your son is missing. I shall look into the problem, beginning right away. I wish I could say that it'll be an easy task, but we all know that it may not be. I don't know this man Slocomb, but that's where I'll start. Miss Chartrell down at the school might also be helpful, or if not she may have some idea of how to better understand Martin. I'll need to be able to talk with you again if I learn anything, so please give me your phone number and address." She handed Ruth Kennedy a piece of paper. "And call me the minute you hear something about your son."

Carol hoped that they would hear something, and that it would be good news. Instinct told her it would not be.

CHAPTER 7

There was nothing to tell Connie Eakins that would be encouraging. But at least she could let her know that she was doing what she had said she would do, hunting for clues that might account for Ernie's disappearance.

"Hello, Mrs. Eakins. I wanted you to know that I'm doing what I can to find your husband. I rode the whole course of the Gravel Grinder with Joe Reiger earlier today, making a special effort to identify places where Ernie might have had trouble or gotten lost. I'm sorry to report that I discovered nothing which looks promising. On the other hand, I now have a much better sense of the route, and I expect to drive it again, taking a few detours which might be helpful. But please don't get your hopes up. I wish I could be more optimistic, but given what little I know, I have trouble imagining that Ernie would have taken any of them."

"I was afraid that this is what you would tell me," Connie said. She was obviously disappointed, but she had gotten herself together and sounded less distraught than she had the day before.

"Are you, like Ernie, a cyclist?" Carol asked.

"Barely, and certainly not in his league."

"So you've never ridden the course your husband was on this week?"

"Never. I'm not nearly as strong as he is, and I can't remember when I last was on an unpaved road."

Carol was pleased to hear her use the present tense, although she was sure that it was from force of habit rather than optimism that Ernie was still alive.

"That's what I thought, but I suppose I was hoping that you might have accompanied him at some time or other on the Gravel Grinder route. Then you might be able to go there with me, maybe see something that looked familiar."

"Oh, I see. Yes, that could be helpful. I'm sorry though. Ernie talks about where he goes on these local rides, but it's all very general. After all, he knows I won't have any idea about the back woods, the hill top areas. It's such a terrible shame, isn't it? He was always talking about how wonderful the little used, rougher roads are. And I wasn't much interested. I preferred the town streets, with their shops, more opportunities to meet up with people I know and enjoy."

"Don't worry. Back roads aren't everybody's thing. Not even mine." It wasn't true. Carol's job put her on many of Cumberland County's back roads. Unfortunately, as her trip with Joe Reiger had made clear, not all of them.

She assured Connie that she would continue to work at finding Ernie and that she hoped he would turn up soon with a convincing explanation for his unexpected disappearance. But she was increasingly of the opinion that Ernie would not resurface, and that if he did she would have nothing to do with it. For all she knew, the Eakins' marriage had been a failure, at least for Ernie, and that it was entirely possible that he had used the occasion of the Gravel Grinder to walk away from it. No, she corrected herself, he might have used the Gravel Grinder to *ride* away from it. Whatever had happened, she would only be going through the motions of finding Ernie. A sad but hardly a dramatic episode in the history of Crooked Lake.

When she hung up the phone, her thoughts immediately turned to what she believed to be a much more important disappearance than that of Ernie Eakins. What had become of Martin Luther Kennedy? She knew logically that the Eakins case was just as important as the Kennedy case. But she was much more troubled by the latter. Perhaps she shouldn't be, but that's the way it was. She hoped that Kevin would understand.

"Kevin, hi, it's me." Carol's call to the cottage came at 2:50 that afternoon. "I know we have plans to go out to dinner, but I'm going to ask you to indulge me and whip up something for supper at home."

"Are you all right?" Kevin sounded worried. Rarely did Carol pass up an opportunity to enjoy a change of pace at the *Cedar Post*.

"I guess so, but I'm not sure. Trouble is, I'd be celebrating, and for some reason I don't feel like celebrating."

"A bad day? All the more reason to take a break. What's the problem?"

"It's too complicated to tell you over the phone. To be honest, I need your input. Don't worry, it's nothing personal, nothing about you and me. Let's just say it's about my moral compass, and that's probably the wrong way to put it. Anyhow, is there enough in the fridge for a light last minute snack? And for what it's worth, I'm not going on the wagon, so put a bottle of wine on ice."

Kevin was still worried, but this was no time to argue about dining at the *Cedar Post*.

"Okay, no problem. The usual time?"

"Yes. I'll be there. It'll be all right."

When Carol arrived home, Kevin knew better than to greet her by reopening the 'cancel the *Cedar Post* discussion.' He gave her a big hug and proceeded to pour two glasses of Chardonnay.

"The deck all right, or would you rather the couch?"

"No matter the circumstances, I'm always in favor of the deck when the sun shines and the temperature is above 75."

"At your service," Kevin said, obviously anxious to tread lightly in what might be a difficult evening.

Five minutes later, wine in hand, they settled into their favorite deck chairs.

"I can tell that you're walking on eggs," Carol said, "so let me put your mind at rest. I love you and I need you. Nothing's the matter except that *two* people have disappeared and I'm expected to find them. But the cases are quite different, or so they appear to me, and I'm having trouble dealing with the way I'm treating them."

"Another missing person? And it's the moral compass issue you mentioned."

"That's probably rather a melodramatic way of putting it, so let me back off and give you the whole story."

CHAPTER 8

Carol had always been comfortable with her evening discussions with Kevin about the day's developments in her profession. He was a good listener and, in spite of an occasionally misplaced sense of humor, frequently quite useful in helping her put a problem in its proper context. But she was still feeling somewhat uncomfortable about the fact that she was approaching the Eakins and Kennedy situations, her two missing persons problems, so differently. Would Kevin see them as she did? And what if he didn't?

Two glasses of wine and a light supper later, Carol had filled Kevin in on her dilemma. Why the view that Ernie Eakins' disappearance was none of the sheriff's business, that it had much to do with the relationship between Ernie and Connie or at the least was something for which there was a solution that didn't involve her? Why the view that Martin Kennedy's disappearance was a problem for the sheriff's department, that finding Martin was her responsibility and an urgent one?

"To be honest," Carol said, "I have the feeling that I'm not being fair to the Eakins, but that it's my heart not my head that's controlling my response to the Kennedy's appeal for help."

"In the first place, you are helping both families. You've just spent the better part of a day driving the route Ernie Eakins rode when he got lost. It's not your fault that you didn't find him. Maybe you feel a greater empathy for the Kennedys, but that doesn't mean that their missing son is your problem and Mrs. Eakins' missing husband is not. In the second place, the heart and the head play very different roles in this body of ours, mine as much as yours. I've never met these people, but I can easily imagine empathizing more with the Kennedys. They've just moved here, they have a sick, retarded child, and to top it all off they're part of a very small minority culture around the lake. They need help in a way that Connie Eakins doesn't."

"That's what I'm afraid I'm thinking. Particularly the cultural thing. I don't want it to look as if I'm patronizing the Kennedys, or maybe that they will think that's what I'm doing. You know, the white authority figure being especially nice to the African-American family out of a sense of white guilt."

"I wouldn't go there, if I were you, Carol. You don't know whether either of these disappearances will turn out to be a criminal matter. It's possible that one of them *will* be the result of a criminal act. Not likely, but possible. I think you're going to have to investigate both cases. But don't confuse your duty as the sheriff with a conviction that we may also have a problem with racism up here in Cumberland County. I know as well as you do that some of the people we know are closet racists, even if they insist they're not. We're not perfect either, and I understand where you're coming from. But my suggestion is that you treat Eakins' disappearance like you're treating Kennedy's. What does it cost you to approach both cases as potential crimes?"

Carol considered her husband's argument. He was right, of course. She might feel better helping the Kennedys solve their problem, but she'd never forgive herself if Ernie Eakins had in fact been the victim of foul play and she had dismissed the possibility.

"I'm persuaded," she said. "Frankly I was pretty sure we'd be on the same page. But it's interesting how the Kennedy story grabbed my attention in a way the Eakins' matter didn't. I guess I've subconsciously thought a lot about the fact that we're living in a white world up here on the lake. And wondering how the few people who come from other cultures are coping. The recent debate about immigration has surely had something to do with it."

"In other words, the US of A is more and more a multicultural society, but Crooked Lake isn't."

"Let's change the subject, okay? We both believe that, all in all, people are decent and caring. I'm making a bet that both Connie Eakins and Martin Kennedy's parents are in the prayers of everyone around the lake."

"I hope you're right. And I'll resist the temptation to mention that we have known some people who aren't decent and caring. You don't need to be reminded that we've had a few murders in recent years."

"There isn't going to be a murder this summer, Kevin!"

"Of course not. Neither of an African-American nor of a cyclist."

Carol was well aware that her assertion that there would be no murder on Crooked Lake this summer might already have been proven wrong. People are always dropping out of sight for reasons much less dire than murder, and she had seen or heard nothing to suggest that Martin Kennedy or Ernie Eakins was a murder victim. On the other hand, both disappearances were unusual and could not be dismissed as 'just one of those things' that happen from time to time. When she sat down with Kevin after supper to talk about the two cases, she had already decided that she would have to investigate both of them. Kevin hadn't changed her mind, but he had strengthened her resolve to treat Ernie Eakins disappearance as seriously as she treated Kennedy's.

By the time she went to bed, she had mapped out her agenda for the following morning. She would find out where Adolph Slocomb lived and then she would pay him a visit.

Slocomb, for whom the retarded and missing African-American boy was working. Her last thought before falling asleep was that she was, perhaps unconsciously, still putting the Kennedys and their problem first, ahead of Connie Eakins.

CHAPTER 9

It was while she was waiting for Officer Byrnes to provide her with the information necessary to get to the Slocomb residence that she realized why she didn't already have it. The Kennedys had never been to where he lived. He had made the agreement to take Martin on at their home, not his, and had subsequently picked him up there and brought him back on each of the few days before he disappeared.

Why, she wondered, had it worked that way? Logically, Slocomb would have wanted the Kennedys to see his place, the place where their son would be spending his days over the summer. And the parents should also have been interested in seeing Martin's work site, especially in view of his problems. Why hadn't they? Or had they, but chosen not to insist on it if Slocomb, for whatever reason, wanted to do it his way. Suddenly, ten minutes after the squad meeting, Carol had another reason why it was important that she meet and talk with Adolph Slocomb. And see where Martin had worked before he disappeared.

Byrnes appeared at her office door with a rough map sketch. Apparently, Slocomb didn't live on any of the main roads or even close to the towns at the end of Crooked Lake's arms.

"Sorry, Carol, but this isn't exactly a triple A map. I didn't bother to give you instructions to get to Southport or onto the east lake road. But once you're up the hill as if you're going to Watkins, I think you'll find the going a bit more of a problem. I had to check with Parsons. He knows the back roads better than I do. Anyway, take a look at my rendition, and then ask me - or one of the other hilltop guys. Maybe you know the area; you grew up here, unlike me. Why anyone would choose to have a place off in the boonies like that, I don't know."

"There are people who think this whole area is the boonies, Tommy. Anyway, thanks for your help. If I get lost, I'll call."

"Who's this guy Slocomb?"

"No idea. Or not much of one. A local family had a son working for him as a handyman, and then the boy went missing. I promised the family I'd look into it, and it seems as if I start by meeting him and seeing what he has to say."

"Probably ran away," Tommy suggested. "Run aways are hard to find until they get homesick."

"Could be, but I suspect it's more complicated than that. If you're interested, I'll let you know what I learn from this man Slocomb, assuming I find him."

"You'll find him. Just follow my map."

Carol chose not to call Slocomb first. She'd gamble that he was at home, and if not at least she'd have found where he lives and thereby simplified the next trip. Locating the man who had hired Martin Kennedy proved to be more difficult than she had expected.

She had driven area roads enough that she was fairly sure she'd be in the general vicinity of Slocomb's home within an hour after leaving Southport. In spite of the map and her earlier ride with Joe Reiger, she soon realized that unmarked dirt tracks frequently led off the bumpy, poorly maintained county road. Joe had not changed direction until he reached the crest of the hill, and it was three miles beyond that point that Tommy"s map called for a right turn when he came to a post marked A.S. 2 m.

She had already gone two miles beyond Tommy's three when she became convinced that she had missed her turn. There was no other traffic, which made turning around and retracing her steps easy. Finding A.S. 2 m. was harder. She soon found herself back at the crest of the hill where Reiger had turned north, and there had been no post at any of the dirt tracks she had passed. Fifteen minutes later Carol knew that all but two of the dirt tracks led to dead ends or only to ruined houses that obviously had not been lived in for years. Which meant either that Slocomb lived on one of the remaining tracks or Officer Byrnes had relied on misinformation.

Carol was soon on a rough washboard of a road that wound its way for several hundred yards until it came to an old house that didn't look much better than the abandoned shacks on the other dirt tracks. She still didn't know that this was where Slocomb lived, but it was obvious that somebody did. A pick-up truck which was much newer than the house and a large shed in front of it told her that. She hoped it was Slocomb's; otherwise it would have been a wasted morning and a frustrated Officer Byrnes.

She parked near the shed and set off for the porch of the house, which looked as if it could collapse if buffeted by a strong wind. As she circled the shed, it became apparent that it was in fact a part of a sprawling pig pen, or, more accurately, a hog pen, because the six animals lying in its muddy interior between the shed itself and a large trough were much too large to be what she though of as pigs. The truth of the matter was that Carol didn't know a pig from a hog, or whether there was a difference between them. But she assumed that Mr. Slocomb, or whoever lived here, was in the business of raising these dirty animals for slaughter and the market.

Her interest in the inhabitants of the pen was quickly replaced by the appearance on the porch of a bearded man wearing a dark rubber apron. He wasn't fat, but he was definitely over weight. Porcine, not surprisingly, was the word that came to her mind.

"What is it that you want, Miss?" he asked. His voice was raspy, as if he were nursing a cold. His face was hard to read. Carol had the feeling, however, that he was not used to company and was probably not happy to see an officer of the law at his doorstep.

"I'm Carol Kelleher, the sheriff of this county, and I'm not sure exactly where I am. I'm looking for Adolph Slocomb. Is that you?"

The man on the porch coughed up some phlegm and spit it out.

"Sorry about that. Nasty sore throat. Yes, I'm Slocomb. Don't have many visitors. What's on your mind?"

"I was hoping to find you, have a talk. This place is hard to find, no mail box, no sign telling me whether there's a house up this track or not. You must not have many neighbors."

"That's for sure," he replied. "What is it you want to talk about?"

"It's complicated. How about we go inside?"

Slocomb coughed again, thought about the sheriff's question.

"As you wish. The house hasn't been picked up in a few days. Why don't you sit on the swing over there, give me ten minutes to put things in order."

"That's not necessary. All I need to do is ask a few questions."

"Doesn't matter. I don't want people to think I keep a rat's nest."

Carol wondered if Slocomb ever had company, and whether he made it a habit to pick up for such company as he did have.

"Well, of course. I'm the visitor. Do what you need to do, just don't feel I need to be impressed."

So this is Adolph Slocomb, she thought as he retreated into the house to make it presentable. Funny looking man, and a funny place for Martin Kennedy to have been working. She found herself wondering what he could have been doing to earn whatever Slocomb paid him. Based on what the Kennedys had told her, it seemed unlikely that he could have been much help with the hogs. What is it anyway that people have to do to raise hogs? In any event, she saw nothing else that justified a handyman. Maybe the inside of the house would provide the answer.

The straightening up of the interior took less than ten minutes.

"Okay," Slocomb said. "It's still no palace, but it will have to do."

Carol followed him into a dark room that had a few places to sit plus a dining room table that still had some dishes on it. At least they were stacked neatly near what was apparently the door to the kitchen. There was no bookcase, much less any books, and the walls were bare. A thoroughly depressing place.

"Here," he said, pointing to a chair which had seen better days but at least looked moderately comfortable. Once she was seated, he moved a dining room chair away from the table and straddled it. She had always hated it when men sat like this, but she hadn't come to Slocomb's home to find fault with his habits.

"Inasmuch as I'm the sheriff, I imagine that you know why I'm here," she said, taking the conversational initiative. "A family named Kennedy has a son who has been working for you. The boy - his name is Martin - recently disappeared. I gather that you called them and reported him missing. His parents are understandably worried about him, and thought that perhaps I could help locate him. What can you tell me about Martin and his disappearance?"

Slocomb leaned forward as if he were having trouble hearing the sheriff.

"Not much," he said. "The boy was with me for less than two weeks and then one day he suddenly wasn't here. I'd picked him up at his parents' place that morning - Monday, I think it was, and he went to work like he usually does. I had to go into town, and when I got back I called out his name and he didn't answer. That didn't surprise me much. He never talked a lot. So I went around the yard, the pen out there, places where he might be. No sign of him. It made no sense, so I drove around a bit, over toward the ravine and back to where Lew Guernsey's road marks the end of my property. Never did find him. I called the Kennedy house, but they must have been at work. So I didn't reach them until evening.

I figured he'd just wandered off, gone home. But if he had, he wasn't there."

No, Carol thought, he almost certainly hadn't gone home - too far, the route too difficult for someone with the problems the Kennedys had described.

"Did you leave Martin alone very often?"

"No. He was a strange boy. I didn't worry much about what he'd do or where he'd go if I wasn't around, but my business was here, not in Yates Center or Southport, or along the lake. I didn't have many reasons for going into town, but that day was an exception."

"What was it that Martin Kennedy did for you?"

Slocomb blew his nose into a large blue handkerchief which looked as if it badly needed a washing.

"Not much, really. He'd bring me coffee, clean up like I just did, once in a awhile help me lug things from the back room down to the pen. Oh, and pump water for the trough, sometimes the kitchen. He didn't have the wits to do much, as the Kennedys probably told you."

Carol didn't wish to tell Slocomb what the Kennedys had told her about their son's problems. But she was puzzled that he had taken this young man on and used him to do what he himself could almost certainly have done easily without help.

"If young Martin wasn't able to be of much help, why did you hire him?"

"In the first place, I didn't get many replies to my call for help. But frankly I felt sorry for him. And for his parents. I guess I thought maybe I could introduce him to the real world. And believe me, my hilltop is the real world, more so than any city, even a small city like Southport. I don't suppose you see it that way, but I do. Always have. Any way, the boy seemed to like what he was doing. He did what he was asked, never complained. I can't imagine what happened to him. Or why."

"You say he was a good worker. Yet you said he was strange. Can you tell me more about that? What do you mean by strange?"

"I'm sure his parents told you he was retarded. Slow to understand what I was telling him, or asking him to do. Probably inherited. You know what I mean. And he had those funny features. Mongoloid, that's the word."

The more Slocomb talked about Martin Kennedy, the more Carol found it hard to picture the arrangement he had worked out with the boy and to understand how it had lasted for as long as it had. Unfortunately, she had never met Martin. Had she done so, his relationship with Slocomb might be easier to understand.

"Did Martin ever say anything that hinted that he might be contemplating running away?"

"Never. He always seemed happy, and I never pushed him to work harder, to do anything which might get him to think about quitting. Why, did his parents tell you something different?"

"No, they didn't. They seem to be as puzzled as I am." It was time to change the subject. "By the way, what is your job?"

"I thought that was obvious. I raise hogs, slaughter them, sell different cuts to stores in the area. It's not a great living, but it lets me live up here where nobody can bother me."

Carol assumed that, without saying so, Slocomb was hinting that her visit was beginning to bother him.

"So, Martin didn't do much, but what he did he did well, or at least he followed instructions and didn't cause you any trouble."

"That's what I said." The hog raiser again sounded as if he were tiring of the sheriff's questions.

"You seem to like it up here, nobody living close by. Although you did mention somebody named Guernsey. Do you ever see him or others who might be called neighbors? It's occurred to me that somebody might have seen Martin. Have you asked around?"

"No, and why should I? Lew's a quarter of a mile away, and there's nobody on the other side, just a wide ravine that the boy wouldn't dare try to cross. He tends to stick to the house and the shed unless I'm with him."

Yes, of course, except that you weren't with him the day he disappeared. Carol decided that she had had enough of Slocomb, a loner whose manner was becoming increasingly unpleasant.

"I think I should be heading for my next appointment." Carol had no other appointment calling her away, but saying she did gave her an excuse to leave. Adolph Slocomb would be happy to have his privacy back. "I hope that young Mr. Kennedy reappears soon, for everybody's sake. Here's my card. Please give me a call if you find him or learn something which might explain what happened to him. In the meanwhile, thanks for your time. If I were you, I'd put up a sign telling visitors that this is the road to your house. As it is, you're really hard to find."

"I'll be doing that, sheriff. Nice talking to you. But sorry I haven't been more help."

Carol considered suggesting that he may have been more help than he realized, but thought better of it. In the first place, it wasn't true. In the second, it might unnecessarily put him on alert.

CHAPTER 10

It was not until Carol was almost back to her office that she had a thought which should have occurred to her an hour or more earlier. Slocomb's residence was very close to the route the Gravel Grinder had followed, only a mile or two beyond where Joe Reiger had turned onto a different road on the hill above the eastern arm of Crooked Lake. What if Ernie Eakins had missed the turn and continued on past the dirt track to Slocomb's place? And had then discovered his mistake. Perhaps he had used the track to turn around. Would Slocomb have seen him? And what if Eakins was having trouble with his bike. Would Slocomb be able to tell her something useful about the other person she was looking for?

Why hadn't the Eakins case come to mind while she was talking with Slocomb? Carol was annoyed with her preoccupation with the Kennedy case, but it was now too late to go back to revisit the reclusive hog farmer. It would, however, be at the top of her agenda tomorrow. Today she would visit the Kennedys and report on her meeting with Slocomb.

It was at 10:40 the next morning that she set off for the Kennedy residence. The Kennedys were anxious to hear about her conversation with Adolph Slocomb, although Henry was worried that asking for the day off to do so might cost him his job at Jefferson's Hardware. But he took the risk and was relieved to discover that the manager was surprisingly sympathetic.

The Kennedy house was roughly a mile south of the downtown area. Carol assumed that its location was due to their limited means. In any event, the house showed its age, needed a paint job, and lacked the shrubs and flower beds which made so much of Southport an attractive village. Ruth was at the door almost as soon as the bell announced Carol's arrival.

"Thank you for searching for Martin," she said. "We hope you learned something encouraging."

"It's too soon to be discouraged. I have seen Mr. Slocomb, talked with him, formed a few impressions. I want to share those with you, and ask you some questions that hadn't occurred to me when we were in my office. What a charming house you have."

And she meant it. It was sparsely furnished, and not in a way that she and Kevin would have chosen. But unlike the exterior, the interior was both fresh and neat. The walls had been painted, the furniture, while traditional, was pleasant and looked comfortable. One wall was devoted to a set of framed photos that provided evidence of a happy extended family; even a boy who was certainly Martin wore a wide smile. Moreover, the Kennedys were obviously readers. A wide wooden bookcase across from the couch said as much.

"Come on in and have a seat. I don't know whether you're a coffee drinker, but I have some that's fresh in the kitchen." Assuming that the sheriff would say yes, Ruth asked if she would like cream and sugar.

"Yes, coffee would be just fine. But I like it black, unsweetened."

Henry Kennedy spoke for the first time.

"I gather that you didn't learn anything that tells us much about Martin's whereabouts. We were hopeful, but not optimistic. You probably were, too."

"I'm afraid so. In my experience, it usually takes time." Carol immediately regretted the pessimism this comment would have conveyed.

"I wish I had good news. But Mr. Slocomb had nothing to say about what might have happened to your son. I do, however, have a better picture of the situation up on the hill where Martin was working."

"What do you mean?" Ruth asked. She was obviously confused as to what the sheriff meant.

"Well, I've now seen where Martin was working, and you haven't. I'm here to tell you about it and why I think you ought to take a trip up to Mr. Slocomb's. I also have had a chance to talk at some length with him, whereas I believe you only met with him when he expressed an interest in hiring Martin. Maybe I'm wrong, but I have assumed you were pleased that he was interested in doing so. Now the situation is different, wouldn't you agree? Of course one of you, perhaps both of you, talked with him when he picked Martin up and brought him home. You did, didn't you?"

It was Henry who knew what Carol had in mind. The Kennedys didn't know Adolph Slocomb as well as she now did, and they should. He was immediately worried that what she had observed and heard was troubling.

"I take it that you saw something, or heard something, from Slocomb that makes you suspicious of him."

"I wouldn't say that. But I would say that he's a strange man. I cannot understand why he needed a handyman. Unless he's not telling me the truth, your son had almost nothing to do. It's possible that in Martin's time there, Mr. Slocomb discovered that Martin wasn't really able to do what he had in mind for him, and that accounts for the very limited load he carried. You know much more than I do about what your son can and cannot do, which is why I think you should go and talk with Mr. Slocomb."

"You're right. We didn't pay enough attention to the situation. Left it too much in Slocomb's hands. I guess we felt so fortunate to have found a place for Martin to spend time out of doors. And Slocomb seemed concerned, a decent man who didn't seem to have any problem hiring a black boy."

"Don't be hard on yourself. Who would have thought this would have happened?" Actually, Carol agreed with Henry that the Kennedys should have been more involved in making the arrangements for their son's summer. But it was too late to change the past.

"So you didn't learn what might have happened to Martin," Ruth said. "What did you learn?"

"Mostly about Slocomb and his dwelling. Sorry. I don't typically call someone's house a dwelling, but where Slocomb lives barely qualifies as a house. It's old, but so is your home and mine. What is unusual is that it serves as living space for both the owner and a bunch of hogs. There's a shed, or a pig pen, semi-detached from the house where he stays, that makes the house part look somewhat like an afterthought. It seems that Slocomb is a farmer, only he raises hogs, not vegetables. All of this is quite a long distance back from the road - you have to take a winding dirt track to get there. I didn't get to estimate how large his property is, but it's big, probably as much as twenty acres. It stretches from a large and deep ravine on one side all the way to another dirt track leading to Slocomb's nearest neighbor on the other."

"He raises hogs?"

"That's what he says. Slaughters them and sells the meat to area stores. Perhaps directly to consumers, although I'm not sure about that."

Ruth grimaced at the thought of Slocomb as a slaughterer of hogs.

"As for the man himself, he's a self described loner. Given where he lives, that seems to be a pretty accurate label. He claims that he rarely leaves the hill house, usually to deliver meat to customers. It was on one of his rare trips to town that Martin disappeared. You've seen him, of course, so you know what he looks like - a rough man, not large but probably strong. I know I've only seen him and talked with him for less than an hour, but he strikes me as a man who is very careful to maintain his privacy. He talked quite a bit about Martin, but almost not at all about himself. Perhaps that's not surprising, inasmuch as I was there to inquire about your son. But I'd guess that he chose his hill top home in part to hide who he is, or was. I wonder when he moved to this area? I should have asked."

"So you are suspicious of Mr. Slocomb. Do you have reason to believe that he has some responsibility for Martin being missing?" It was Henry who asked the question.

"No, nothing I heard from him, nothing in his manner, suggested that that's the case. I'm only telling you what I observed and my impression of him. Like I've said, he's a strange man. That doesn't mean he could be a factor in Martin's disappearance. So please don't look at it that way because you think I do. What I'm anxious to have you do is visit Slocomb, ask him lots of questions, try to get a sense of the relationship he was developing with your son. How do you think Martin would have reacted to Slocomb? Would he have expected him to talk to him, to act interested in him, or would he have been happy to be working for someone who said little, a man who gave him jobs to do and otherwise left him alone? My problem, as must be obvious to you, is that I don't begin to know enough about Martin to know how he would have reacted to someone like Slocomb. Is your son, too, a loner? How do you suppose he would process instructions from Slocomb? How would you suspect he would deal with that environment?"

"Off hand, I don't think we could answer those questions. But we'll take your advice and visit the hog farmer. And I'll try very hard to keep an open mind, even if it isn't easy. Ruth, too."

"Good. And I promise to stay in touch. You'll do the same, won't you?"

"Oh yes, and thank you for standing by," Ruth said.

Carol gave them a road map she had sketched, hoping they would be able to find Slocomb's without too much trouble. Then she did what she almost never did in the course of an investigation. She leaned over and kissed Ruth.

CHAPTER 11

The car radio was tuned to a local channel, although the sheriff's mind was still on the Kennedys' problem. It was not until the announcer, Ben Barber, a better DJ than a news reporter, said something about a lake accident that Carol turned her attention to the radio voice. Barber was talking about someone who had hit his head on the dock while somersaulting into the lake. She thought Barber had mentioned a name, but she had missed it because her thoughts had been on Martin Kennedy's parents. What had gotten her attention was word that the injured diver was in a local hospital and that his carelessness just might have resulted in a serious injury.

Boys will be boys, she thought; she hoped that this one would be okay, that he had learned a lesson rather than caused his family sleepless nights as Martin had. But the accident was apparently important enough that it warranted more than a twenty second reference. So Barber, who obviously had few facts at his disposal, repeated the victim's name and the hospital where he was presumably recovering.

"All we know is that Maurice Heaslip is now at St. Agnes Hospital. We will keep you posted when we have more information. Now back to Music Through the Years, this time one of Nat King Cole's famous hits, 'Mona Lisa.'" Carol turned the radio off and let her thoughts return to the Kennedys. She had never heard of Heaslip.

She had not been back at the office more than fifteen minutes when JoAnne told her she had a call from Joe Reiger. What would the Chamber of Commerce man want of her? Perhaps he had learned something about the Eakins case. She hoped so.

"Hi, Joe. I hope this a good news call."

"I'm afraid not. At least it has nothing to do with Eakins. But we do have another problem with one of the Gravel Grinder riders. It's not that somebody else is missing, and you may not be interested. But another cyclist is in trouble. Name's Maurice Heaslip. He's not even a Crooked Lake guy. Home's in South Dakota and for some reason he came east for our event. Just thought you might find it interesting that the Gravel Grinder seems to be taking a toll on its participants." Joe chuckled.

"I just heard about this man Heaslip on the radio. Banged his head doing a crazy dive off a dock somewhere. Sorry your call doesn't tell us about Eakins. Do you know Heaslip? Did you even know he rode in your race? Not a race, but you know what I mean."

"I met him briefly. Probably talked for three minutes, long enough to know he's from the Dakotas. He seems to spend much of his spare time traveling the country for things cyclists do. But hearing about him gave me an excuse to do something I should have done before. I made a copy of my list of who was in the Gravel Grinder - thought you might be interested in it. Mostly locals, or at least Finger Lakes types."

"Thanks, Joe. You're suggesting I get off my butt and start interviewing well over a hundred people, a few of them not even from around here. One of them now in the hospital. You want to help?"

"Not really. That's why I'm giving you a list of those who rode last week. But of course I'll pass along anything I hear that could help you find Eakins."

"Like Maurice Heaslip's accident, right?"

"Okay, score one for our sheriff. No, Heaslip had nothing to do with Eakins going missing. Remember, he's from South Dakota."

Carol had an idea, or rather a question.

"What's a guy who came all the way from South Dakota for the Gravel Grinder doing on Crooked Lake a week afterwards? You'd think he'd have headed home or off to Colorado or someplace else for another ride. I think I'll make a trip over to St. Agnes."

"That's interesting," Joe said. "Maybe he's got friends or family here. Maybe that's why he came to our Gravel Grinder - kill two birds with one stone."

"That's probably what happened." Carol agreed with Reiger, but she still intended to pay the careless diver a visit. If he was still in the hospital. And after she'd gone back to Adolph Slocomb's to see if he'd seen Eakins during the Gravel Grinder. That was much more important than looking in on a citizen of South Dakota who was spending the week on Crooked Lake.

Carol spent much of the next hour thinking about her priorities. And more importantly about the task of interviewing more than one hundred cyclists who had accompanied Ernie Eakins on the recent Gravel Grinder. Heaslip was the least of her worries. How on earth was she going to talk to so many locals, most of whom would know Eakins, many of whom would be his friend?

Not surprisingly, one thought led to another. Why had she let herself become so entangled in an issue which was unlikely to have anything to do with maintaining law and order in Cumberland County? This was a question which had been bothering her for more than a week. She thought about it as she drove back to the cottage at the end of the day, but she already knew the answer: she was not only a law enforcement professional, she was also a human being with a strong moral compass. Now she would have to add Joe Reiger's long list of cyclists who had participated in the Gravel Grinder to the search for Ernie Eakins and Martin Kennedy.

CHAPTER 12

That evening passed without a word about the disappearance of either Martin Kennedy or Ernie Eakins. Carol, for a change, was in no mood to bring her problems home. Instead they took a leisurely canoe ride and played scrabble until she excused herself to take a shower and retire early. Kevin wondered why the nighttime shower instead of her usual one in the morning, but knew his wife well enough not to ask if everything was all right.

The next morning was very much the same, although she was out of bed and through breakfast first.

"Don't worry about me," she said as she leaned over his half asleep figure and gave him a kiss before leaving for the office. "I'll be fine."

Carol had no idea whether she would in fact be fine. Too much depended on matters that were beyond her control. One of those matters would occupy her morning. Did Adolph Slocomb happen to see Ernie Eakins during the Gravel Grinder? Or, to approach the issue differently, had Eakins lost his way or had a problem with his bicycle which took him down the track to Slocomb's house on the hill east of Crooked Lake? She doubted that Slocomb would be of any help, but she had to revisit the hog farmer and ask the question. And then she had to take a trip to the St. Agnes Hospital and see how Maurice Heaslip was doing. Should she ask him why he had come all the way from South Dakota to spend a day riding Cumberland County's rough roads? The very fact that she asked herself that question irritated her. It was none of her business, and certainly had nothing to do with the disappearance of two local residents.

She spent less than half an hour at the office, told JoAnne where she would be, and headed back to Slocomb's. This time she had no trouble finding her way. She had decided that it would not be necessary to call ahead; she would park at the hog pen and make her way directly to the front door.

"Hey, what are you doing?" It was Mr. Slocomb, who came rushing out of the pen as Carol climbed the steps to the house.

"Good morning, Mr. Slocomb. I was hoping to see you."

"Well, here I am. But people don't go into my house without my permission. I know you're the sheriff, but I have rights, too."

"I wasn't planning to barge into the house, just knock on the door. There were some questions I forgot to ask when I was here the other day. Glad to find you at home."

"What do you want? I told you all I know about young Kennedy."

"I may be interrupting your morning chores, but if you'll give me twenty, twenty five minutes, I'll head back to Cumberland. Those hogs must be demanding."

"They are. They keep me busy. Now, if you'll just take a seat over there, I'll neaten up for you. Please try to remember that the hogs tend to be impatient."

So it's going to be deja vu all over again, Carol thought Why this necessity of neatening up? His efforts on her earlier visit had hardly made the living room where they sat and talked a particularly pleasant place to be. In any event, Carol once again took a porch seat and waited.

"Now, what is it this time? Unfortunately, the boy hasn't turned up. I'm guessing that he's wandered off somewhere. Maybe you should put a notice in the papers or use the TV."

Carol had already decided to do what Slocomb had suggested, but not until her officers had combed the ravine to the south of Slocomb's property.

"I'm still worried about Martin Kennedy, as are his parents. Incidentally, I've urged them to come up and meet with you."

"You have?" He didn't sound pleased with what the sheriff had suggested. "That's not necessary. I've told them all I know. I don't want my place to become a hunting ground for wandering children."

"Look, I'm not here to discuss the Kennedy disappearance, much as it troubles me. I'm here to talk about somebody else who's disappeared. Have you heard about the man who didn't come back from a bike hike last week? Actually, it wasn't a hike, but a popular annual race of sorts, something they call the Gravel Grinder. You must have heard about it. It's always a big event."

"Gravel Grinder? Never heard about such a thing. Why are you asking me about it?"

"Because the route the cyclists were on took them not far from your house."

"I'm not following you. Surely nobody planned a race up my road. They'd need my permission, and they wouldn't get it. Besides, who in his right mind would want to ride up a rough dirt road like mine."

"I'm sure the people who planned the event didn't intend to send the cyclists up your road. But the Gravel Grinder is designed to give participants a challenging day. They ride for hours over bad rural roads, not paved ones. I thought there was a possibility that this rider who went missing got lost and found himself on your road. Maybe you saw him."

"Well, I didn't. I don't even know what day you're talking about, not that it matters. I've never seen a bike or a bike rider on my property since I moved here. So why don't you let me get back to my hogs."

"Didn't you tell me that you went into town one day? It was the day young Kennedy disappeared. That was the day of the Gravel Grinder."

"So what? If I wasn't here, how the hell was I to see a cyclist on my property?"

"I'm simply trying to track down the guy who never got back from his ride that day. It's not likely, but he may have taken the wrong road - yours, or maybe the one on the property north of you. What did you say his name is?"

"Lew Guernsey. But why don't you ask him. It's pretty obvious that I know nothing about this cycling nonsense. And I do have to take care of my hogs. Glad to see you, but I'm in no position to help you find a bunch of missing persons."

Carol let herself out. Slocomb followed her to the yard and disappeared into the shed. It was clear that he preferred the company of filthy hogs to that of an inquisitive sheriff.

Her feelings about the hog farmer were somewhat different than they had been on her first visit. For one thing, he had been less pleasant. Perhaps it had just been a bad day, and he had already made it clear that he didn't like company. But today he had been conspicuously annoyed by her intrusion on his life. Then there had been the unnecessary routine of straightening up the house before admitting her. The results were not only unimpressive; they were impossible to see. It was as if he had cleaned nothing up, only removed something which he didn't wish her to see. But what had bothered her most wasn't what he had said and how he had said it, but the look which had come over him when she told him why she had taken another trip to the hilltop house. His reaction was not dramatic. In fact, it was barely noticeable. But Carol had been in the business of observing body language and slight changes of expression for too long not to be aware that

Adolph Slocomb was not hearing about the Gravel Grinder and the missing cyclist for the first time.

As she drove back to the office, Carol tried to make sense of what she had seen and heard at Slocomb's. She had no luck. The hog farmer could not possibly have played any role in Martin Kennedy's disappearance. He had been in town; Kennedy had been at the hilltop house. Similarly, he could not possibly have had anything to do with Eakins' disappearance for the same reason. Once more she found herself wondering why she was investing so much of her time on these problems, neither of which was typical of a sheriff's responsibilities.

And now she was on her way to a hospital to see someone else whose problem was even less a part of a sheriff's job description.

CHAPTER 13

Maurice Heaslip was dozing when she walked into his room at St. Agnes. He looked to be about forty years of age, but his looks may have been deceiving due to the fact that his face was discolored and unshaven. A beige colored blanket covered much of his body, making it difficult to guess his height and weight. Probably five ten or eleven and close to two hundred pounds. No nurse or tech on the floor had tried to dissuade Carol from visiting Heaslip, which indicated that he was presumably in good enough condition to leave the hospital soon, perhaps that afternoon.

It was while Carol was making up her mind whether to take the chair in the corner and wait for Heaslip to wake up that he opened his eyes and stared at his unannounced visitor. He said nothing, but the expression on his face suggested that he was surprised to see an officer of the law at his bedside.

"Hello, Mr. Heaslip. How are you doing?" she asked.

"I'm fine, if somewhat annoyed with myself for doing something so foolish. Who are you?"

"I'm the sheriff of this county, and I dropped by to see if you're making progress and getting ready to go home."

"I thought sheriffs nabbed speeders, not paid courtesy calls to hospital patients."

"We also welcome visitors, and rumor has it that you've come all the way from South Dakota. Sorry that your stay here has been spoiled by the accident."

"That's nice of you, but forgive me for assuming that you may have some other reason for paying me a visit."

"Fair enough. I really did drop by to see how you're doing. But to be completely honest, I'm here to discuss the Gravel Grinder bicycle event, which I understand you participated in. I didn't know cyclists travelled so far to do that."

Heaslip didn't immediately comment on her attempt to leaven the conversation with a bit of humor. When he did, he said what Kevin had told her he would say.

"You must not be a serious cyclist, sheriff. Those of us who are spend a lot of our time - some would probably say too much of it - going from place to place to do what a lot of people did in your jurisdiction last week. If I hadn't been here, I'd have been in Arkansas or Vermont. I suppose you could call it an obsession, or at least a habit. I enjoy riding a bicycle of one type or another as often as I can, in one place or another."

"How did you know that there was a race or whatever you call it in New York's western finger lakes?"

Heaslip laughed.

"That's easy. Every interest, every hobby, has magazines, papers, websites that tell their fans and followers what's going on and where. I bet that your Gravel Grinder was advertised, maybe even featured, in a dozen or more publications, and that hundreds of people like me subscribe. In any event, I spotted the news that there was to be a Gravel Grinder around Crooked Lake and decided I would like to take part."

"Your trip to our lake had nothing to do with friends or relatives who live here?"

Heaslip's smile disappeared.

"Why would you think that? I wasn't the only one from somewhere else. Met a guy from Kentucky. Never asked him if he grew up here, but I'd be surprised if he did. Cyclists go where they can ride with others who get their kicks from the same thing."

"Did you hear about one of the riders who disappeared somewhere along the route? Never crossed the finish line. Everyone's talking about it. Seems it's never happened before."

"That's unusual. No, I hadn't heard about it. I'd probably been stuck here in the hospital before the news spread around town."

"His name's Eakins. We're asking around, and I thought you might have met him."

"I doubt it. Of course I talked with a lot of the guys, but you don't get a chance to make a list of who you meet."

Carol was surprised that Heaslip hadn't heard about the cyclist who'd gone missing.

"I take it you didn't stick around Southport for what comes afterwards. Word is it's the best part of the day. You'd have enjoyed it."

Heaslip chose not to respond to what sounded like a criticism.

Carol had stopped at St. Agnes to pay her respects to a visitor who'd had an accident, not to question him about his presence on Crooked Lake, but she found herself doing just that.

"Well, we must have made a good impression, you staying on here for a few days. Where was it you stayed and had your accident?"

"Look, sheriff, I don't wish to be unpleasant, but my head hurts and I'd like to get some sleep. I would like to head back to Rapid City, but they're concerned about my concussion and they're not ready to discharge me yet."

"I didn't mean to wake you up, Mr. Heaslip. I'm sorry that your trip east ended this way. Good luck." Carol gave him a warm smile and backed out of room 406 on the observation floor.

She climbed into her car in the shaded parking lot in front of the hospital, but didn't put her key in the ignition. Instead she sat behind the wheel and took a drink of the now warm ice tea beside her seat. Why was her visit with Maurice Heaslip bothering her? He had had a concussion, was not feeling well, needed to be left alone rather than subjected to questions by a sheriff who had no reason to be asking him why he had come to Crooked Lake for a bicycle event and stayed at a local B & B after it had ended. Had she become so obsessed with her job that she had to treat everyone as if he were somehow involved in whatever case was worrying her? Heaslip had said nothing that justified the fact that she had turned a thoughtful visit into an irrelevant Q and A.

On the other hand, why *had* he come all the way from the Black Hills of western South Dakota to New York's Finger Lakes to ride a bicycle. She knew that cyclists loved to ride and were known to do it often and everywhere from city streets to rough country roads. But so far from home, in a place not as spectacular as one's own backyard, without one's friends? She wished - or did she? - that Kevin was a cyclist, someone who could tell her what it was like to have that kind of a hobby.

CHAPTER 14

Maurice Heaslip stepped out of bed and went to the window where he could see the hospital parking lot two stories below him. As he had expected, the sheriff appeared and went to a police car in the second row. He went back to his bed and stretched out for what he assumed would be one last time. The doctor had told him that he would be discharged as soon as one more report came back from the lab, and he expected it to be a good one. For the fourth or fifth time since entering the hospital he vowed he would not again pretend to be a swimmer, much less a diver, things he almost never did in western South Dakota.

Why had the sheriff paid him this visit? Was her schedule so blank that she had time to be a good samaritan? Or did she know something about him that brought her to his bedside? But no, that was unlikely. How could she possibly know anything about him except that he was from South Dakota and had come east to be in a Gravel Grinder? While waiting for the doctor's report and the discharge from the hospital, Heaslip thought about what had happened in Rapid City and what had brought him to Crooked Lake.

It had been two years ago, and the occasion had been another cycling event. Not a Gravel Grinder this time, but a race in the Black Hills. There had been many more participants, certainly many more from out of state. His wife, Gladys, was also a cyclist, and she enjoyed taking in visitors who had come to Rapid City to participate in events. He had had no idea how many had inquired about sharing their spare room or why the one who did so had lucked out. In any event the man who had stayed for three nights at the Heaslip house was Ernie Eakins, a good looking guy who had brought two bikes with him, apparently to give him an option after testing tracks which he had never ridden before.

Eakins was an experienced cyclist and a pleasant guest. They had talked a lot, exchanging information about the very different regions of the country where they lived. Ernie had been complimentary of the Black Hills and Mt. Rushmore and thought his host would find the Finger Lakes equally interesting. But he had also been other than a welcome guest, or so Maurice had decided afterthe race was over and Eakins had returned to New York state. The problem was initially masked by the fact that Eakins talked almost exclusively about cycling, which he obviously enjoyed or, as he said on several occasions, spent almost every weekend doing.

But it had soon become apparent that biking wasn't the only thing on Eakins' mind. His other interest was Gladys Heaslip. Up to a point this was understandable and harmless. Gladys was an attractive woman with a good sense of humor and a welcoming manner which made everyone feel at home in her presence. Never before had Maurice felt that his marriage was even remotely challenged. That changed in three days, and it changed without anything being said or done. At first Maurice was surprised by his reaction to what he thought was happening. But once it had taken root under his skin, it would not go away. And it became an obsession when an embarrassingly friendly thank you note from Eakins to Gladys arrived ten days later.

Just what was it that had alerted him to Eakins' interest in his wife? And to the possibility that she might possibly find him more interesting, more attractive, than he could have believed she would? He had run this through his mind many times, and the answer always had something to do with eyes. It wasn't just that they looked at each other so much. People do that when they talk. It was the look in those eyes. He'd read enough novels to know that authors were always giving eyes the most important role in descriptions of facile expressions. He had frequently found this device annoying, but now he wasn't so sure. Too often while Eakins was sharing their house his eyes and Gladys's were doing more than looking at each other. They were communicating with each other in a very personal way, a way which managed to exclude everyone else in the room.

He had never asked Gladys what was going on, and she had never mentioned it. Eakins had never touched her, as far as he knew, or acted as if he might. On the surface, they were simply new acquaintances who were pleased to be enjoying each other's company. But Maurice was unable to shed the thought that his wife had a wandering eye, and that Ernie Eakins was to blame.

And so it was that he made a decision to come to the Gravel Grinder on Crooked Lake. His plan was to avoid letting Eakins know he was coming but to surprise him somewhere on the trail which they would be following out of the small town of Southport. It had gone exactly as he had intended it should until he decided to extend his trip and take a swim that turned into a minor disaster.

CHAPTER 15

Ruth and Henry Kennedy were, for the first time, nearing the turn in the road which the sheriff had told them led to Adolph Slocomb's house, the place were their son had worked. Neither of them was happy to be doing what they were doing. In the first place, they were feeling guilty that they had not visited Slocomb before they agreed to let Martin work for him. Visiting him now could look as if they might be inclined to blame him for their son's disappearance. Henry had actually said as much, although he wasn't sure why he was considering that possibility.

In spite of the discomfort both were feeling, they were determined to follow the sheriff's advice.

"We have to turn here," Ruth said. "It must be under a mile. Do you hope he's not at home? I do."

"No. We've come all this way, and if we don't catch him now we'll have to come back tomorrow. I'm nervous, too, but we're doing it for Martin's sake. I keep telling myself that the man was doing us a favor."

"I know, but -" Martin's mother couldn't bring herself to finish what she wanted to say.

Five minutes later they were driving down a rough road toward what looked like a windowless one story shack. Neither said anything, but both of the Kennedys were experiencing an increasingly acute anxiety about what lay ahead.

"At least there is a house," Henry said as they came closer to the shack and the building which stood behind it. "It looks an awful lot like that old picture of my great, great grandfather's slave quarters."

"What did we let ourselves in for?" It was Ruth's question, but she didn't expect an answer.

"Maybe we turned at the wrong place."

"I don't think so. That's Mr. Slocomb, coming around from the back of the shack."

The man approaching their car was wearing dirty overalls, a plaid shirt and grey rubber boots. His face made it clear that he was not in a good mood.

"Now let's stop right there!" It was a loud voice and an unpleasant one. Slocomb had not recognized the people in the car.

Henry stopped the car and opened the door and stepped out.

"Good morning, Mr. Slocomb. We're Martin's parents. Our son was working for you until he got lost."

Slocomb stopped in his tracks, but he continued to look unpleasant, perhaps even more-so.

"You're the Kennedys, right?"

"We are, and we thought we'd pay you a visit, see if you've learned anything more about our son."

"I'd have been in touch if I had anything to tell you." Then, as if suddenly aware that he owed the Kennedys a more pleasant welcome, he expressed his regret that the boy hadn't turned up.

"I was afraid that that was the case," Henry Kennedy said, "but we thought we'd at least get a chance to see where Martin was spending his days."

Slocomb's scowl returned.

"You want to see the house? That's not a good idea. I don't keep a neat place like you do. I'm a bachelor, you know."

"We don't worry about being neat. You've employed our son, that's what matters."

The Kennedys were closer to the porch than Slocomb, and the front door was wide open. Henry started up the steps, while Ruth pulled at his shirt cuff.

"Don't be impolite," she whispered. "Let him straighten the place up first."

"No." Henry said, "I'm doing it my way." He turned to the man who had employed their son for a little more than a week. "Don't worry. We just have to sit down. It's the heat, you know."

"Now, just wait a minute. This is my house, and I make the rules around here." Slocomb, who hadn't been particularly pleasant since their arrival, was obviously angry.

"Like I said, there's no reason for you to worry about us. None at all. What we'd like to do is see where Martin stayed when he worked here, what the job required. Maybe we'll get some kind of idea what happened to him. Ruth and I still can't imagine him simply disappearing."

"Are you accusing me of causing his disappearance?" Slocomb was hurrying toward the porch, determined to beat the Kennedys into the house. But he was too late because the front door was wide open.

"We won't be long, I promise. Just a look around, a question or two, then we'll be gone. I know you're busy and -" Suddenly he stopped his half-hearted apology for their intrusion.

"My God, what is that?" He was looking right at a large framed poster which occupied much of the space above the couch which faced the door.

"What's the matter?" Ruth had never heard her husband talk like that.

"There!" He pointed at the wall over the couch. "What a terrible thing to have in your living room. It's a Nazi picture!"

Slocomb was now with them in the living room. The three of them were staring at a large poster, the right hand side containing a large swastika, and left hand side a portrait of Adolph Hitler, arm raised in the Nazi salute.

"Now you just wait a minute. You had no business coming in here without me, and what I'm sure you're thinking is nothing but nonsense. I'm not a Nazi lover, I'm a United States citizen. But since you barged into my house without permission, you should let me tell you about that poster. If it bothers you so much, perhaps we should sit in the kitchen." Slocomb brushed past the Kennedys, leading the small parade of upset people away from this reminder of the worst war in history.

Henry Kennedy, shocked and horrified by what he had seen and what Martin had surely seen as well, wanted to leave immediately. Ruth was as upset as her husband, but was anxious to hear Slocomb's story of the offensive picture which had been part of their son's everyday life for a week.

Seated at the kitchen table, the Kennedys tried to swallow their shock and let Slocomb talk about the poster in his living room. The owner of the hilltop house was equally upset, but he realized that the Kennedys would spread the word about what they had seen unless he persuaded them that the poster had a totally different history.

"Like I said, the poster isn't what you think. Well, of course it's a poster, but it says nothing about my views." Slocomb stared at the couple across the table from him. He was obviously both uncomfortable and searching for words that would calm these strangers. And they were strangers, people he had never made any effort to get to know. "Now just relax and I'll tell you what it really is. It's something I got when my Uncle Ben died. He was in the US army in WW II, and among the troops on the western front in the closing days of the war. His unit was in a small town that fortunately had escaped serious damage, and they were resting from a march, or maybe it was a battle, in a little church. Ben told me he'd gotten up to go take a leak when he spotted this poster stuck on a stone wall near where they observed mass. He thought he'd take a souvenir home with him, so he ripped it off the wall, folded it up and stuck it in his knapsack. Like I said, he gave it to me just before he died. That's the story. For me it was a memento of the war. I was too young to go over there and fight, so my uncle gave me something to remember it by."

"But why hang it in your house?" Henry asked. "It's also a reminder of that horrible Nazi regime. They killed millions, including thousands of Americans. Why honor them?"

"I'm not honoring them, Mr. Kennedy. All I'm doing is remembering who they were, what they did. And why are you so upset by what they did? What did your own government do back then? It lynched people like you, treated you just like Hitler did his people. Maybe I should replace my poster with a picture of slaves like your grandparents, sweating in the cotton fields and hanging from a rope in a tree. I'll bet you wouldn't like that any better."

Neither Henry nor Ruth knew what to say to this unexpected analogy. They knew the slavery story, of course, and had spent time working for an organization that sought reparations for it. But they had never spoken in terms like Slocomb's.

Their meeting with Slocomb proved to be much shorter than they had expected. He obviously hadn't tried very hard to welcome them to his house, and they had been exceedingly uncomfortable to be there. When they left, the Kennedys did their best to thank him for his time, but they knew they had not convinced him that they meant it.

"What a disaster," Henry said to his wife as they drove back to Southport. "Why didn't we pay more attention? Martin might still be with us if we'd done our homework."

"Do you think so? Do you think Martin's disappearance is Mr. Slocomb's fault? I didn't like the man, but I have trouble imagining that he caused Martin to run away."

"Maybe, maybe not. But Slocomb, he's a terrible man to leave your only child with. And what a place. We should have insisted on going up there and seeing where Martin would have been working, what he'd be doing. I'll never be able to get that Nazi poster off my mind. Can you imagine such awful taste?"

"You think Mr. Slocomb is himself a Nazi type, don't you?"

"Yes, I do. No decent man would put something like that up on his living room wall. It's an affront to all African-Americans."

"We don't really know that. He says it's just something his uncle brought home from the war, not something he believes in."

"Please, Ruth, don't buy into what he says. I'm sure he's lying."

"I know that the Nazis hated the Jews. We don't know that they also hated people like us."

Henry reacted to her suggestion by flooring the pedal.

"Yes we do! Remember the '30s olympics and the reaction to the victories of our Jesse Owens. Those victories made a mockery of Hitler's crude talk about the supremacy of the Aryan race. And there on his wall we still have Hitler."

"Please slow down dear."

"Okay, if you'll stop making excuses for Slocomb. His story about the uncle on the Western front, for example. A big lie! Where did this uncle get his poster? In a church. How likely is that? I know that some German churches supported Hitler, but isn't it strange that uncle Slocomb or whatever his name was happened on this tribute to the Nazis right next to where local Christians came to pray."

"Maybe this was one of the bad churches that preferred Hitler to the Bible," Ruth suggested.

Henry was beginning to be annoyed with his wife's attempt to be rational.

"Why are you so ready to defend Slocomb?"

"I'm not defending him. He's not a nice man. But fifteen minutes in his grubby house doesn't make him a neo-Nazi."

"No? Then how do you account for his phony story about the poster?"

"How do you know that it's phony?"

"It's easy. He either made it up as he went along or he'd rehearsed it to use in situations like the one we just walked into. Think about it. He says that his uncle found the poster on a church wall in 1945, or maybe it was 1944. He claims he took it off the wall, folded it up, and stuffed it in his rucksack. In other words, the poster is very old and was inevitably carried around in a crowded back pack for months. Now what did the poster in Slocomb's look like? How about neat, clean, not creased. That's what we saw. I'll bet anything that the poster was made recently by some firm that does things like that for neo-Nazis, right wing advocates for white people who hate Jews, African-Americans, anyone they find unacceptable. Now why did Slocomb make up that story about his uncle's poster?"

Ruth didn't say anything. She looked thoughtful, then worried.

"So you think he's really one of those white racists, maybe a member of some kind of a Nazi party?"

"I don't follow stories about such people, but I suspect there's a Nazi party right here in our country. Probably a KKK party, too. The FBI would know; I don't. But there are surely people who have views like that. And I'm pretty sure one of them was employing our

Martin. The sheriff urged us to talk with Slocomb. She never called him a racist, much less a Nazi, but I would't be surprised if she thinks so."

CHAPTER 16

They had made no plans to call the sheriff as soon as they got back home, but Henry was too anxious to let her know what they had discovered to postpone that call. Did their experience correspond with hers? Or was he jumping to an unwarranted conclusion because of the offensive poster?

Instead of dropping Ruth off and heading back to the hardware store, Henry parked the car and headed into the house and to the telephone. Unfortunately, the sheriff was not at her desk.

"When do you expect her?" he asked, doing his best not to sound frustrated.

"I can't be sure," JoAnne replied. "Is there a message I can leave for her? She's very likely to come back to the office before calling it a day, but she didn't give me any details about her afternoon plans."

"Look, this is Henry Kennedy. My wife and I have been up to see Adolph Slocomb, as the sheriff urged us to do. It was an important meeting, as she assumed it would be. To be completely honest, it was a horrible meeting, one I need to talk about with the sheriff. Can you have her call me as soon as she comes in?"

"Where can she reach you, at home or at work, Mr. Kennedy?"

A necessary question, and one he didn't have a ready answer for. If he were at the store, Ruth would take the call. But much as he was confident that she would report the facts, he wasn't sure she would sound as distressed as he would. Perhaps he should stay at the house.

"I'll be at home, and I'm sure she has our number. Please tell her it's very important."

As it happened, Carol didn't call the Kennedys until twenty minutes to five, by which time Henry was very close to a nervous wreck, in spite of Ruth's efforts to calm him down.

The sheriff knew at once that she was talking to a very anxious man, someone who had more on his mind than the fact that his son had gone missing. As if that weren't enough.

"Thank you, sheriff. I was afraid I wouldn't hear from you until tomorrow. Ruth and I spoke with Mr. Slocomb today, and we are very upset. And that's putting it mildly."

"I'm sorry not to have called back sooner. Would it help if I came by your house instead of hearing what you have to say over the phone?"

"Oh, yes, if it isn't too inconvenient."

"Then I'll do it. I'll be on my way in about five minutes." It was a worried sheriff who set off for Southport.

Carol had known that the Kennedys would not like the Slocomb home, the hogs, the man's coarse and abrupt manner. But Henry had sounded as if the situation was even worse. Had they learned something that told them that Martin was dead or more likely to be dead? Had Slocomb declined to see them? Had he seen them but been rude, even indifferent to their problem? By the time she had reached the Kennedy home she was nearly as nervous as Henry had sounded over the phone.

She wasn't surprised to find both Mr. and Mrs. Kennedy sitting on the front porch where they could see the official car as it turned the corner and came to a stop in front of them.

"So glad you're here, sheriff." Henry did, in fact, look and sound grateful. Carol was immediately conscious of the fact that he had decided to take charge of the conversation. Or that Ruth had chosen to let him do so.

"Let's go inside. I'd rather not talk about this out here in front of our neighbors."

Carol had no problem with going inside, and she could understand his reluctance to be seen talking with the sheriff. But she sensed that something else was going on.

"Do you care for tea or coffee?" Ruth asked. "We've brought you clear down here, the least we can do is give you something to drink."

"No thanks," Carol said. She'd wait for a glass of wine with Kevin when she got home, assuming that the Kennedys' report on their meeting with Slocomb did not necessitate an unexpected change in her evening plans.

The conversation dealt with routine matters until Ruth returned with the tea, at which time Henry brought up the issue which had led to the urgent request that they meet with the sheriff.

"You will want to know how our session with Slocomb went. The answer is not well. But there's an even more important matter, an alarming one. You didn't bring it up when you urged us to visit him at his house on the hill, and I'm sure you had your reasons for not doing so. But let me ask a question. When you visited him, you must have seen the big poster on his living room wall. Did you ask him abut it?"

"Forgive me, but I'm puzzled. There was no poster on the living room wall. I don't remember any pictures in the living room, or anywhere else. I take it that you saw one, however. It obviously got your attention. Tell me about it."

Carol was surprised by Henry's question. She had expected something about the hog pen, Slocomb's impatience, his reluctance to receive visitors. She also found it hard to believe that he had taken the time to suddenly put up a poster or picture in a house that had only had bare walls when she had been there.

"Well, I'm as surprised that you saw no pictures as you obviously are that I saw that awful poster," Henry said. "Something unusual going on up there, I'd say. Okay, this is what we saw, and it really shocked us. Ruth and I think it would have shocked you, too. It was a poster about as big as that window over there, and it was a Nazi poster, half of it a giant swastika, the other half a picture of Hitler, arm raised in that familiar Nazi salute."

Henry Kennedy paused to see how the sheriff would react to this information. She was obviously surprised. No, that was too mild a word. As he had said, she was shocked.

"Like I said, this is news to me." Carol was trying to understand what it meant, where Slocomb would have gotten the poster, why he had put it up on his living room wall. She hadn't cared for the man, but this news changed her picture of him dramatically. Yet how, she didn't know. And then something came to her.

"Did Mr. Slocomb ask you to stay out of the house until he had a chance to straighten it up?"

"Sort of," Henry said. "I don't think he wanted us to be in the house, but we were already on the porch and the door was open, so we went on in. And immediately saw the poster, couldn't miss it."

"So you saw his living room before he'd had a chance to go in and neaten it up?"

"He didn't mention cleaning the place up, but he seemed to be annoyed that we wanted to see where Martin had been working. We weren't trying to be rude, but like I said, we were right there at the door."

"Then your situation was unlike mine. When I was there, he insisted I let him straighten the house before he'd let me in. And the front door was always closed until he'd done so. When I went in, there was nothing on the wall over the couch. I always thought he didn't need to worry about neatening the place up, and frankly it never looked as if he'd done much neatening before I went in. I never knew there was a poster on the wall, so it never occurred to me that neatening up meant taking a poster off the wall so I wouldn't see it."

"It sounds as if he was trying to hide that poster."

"It certainly does. This is a new development, and frankly it surprises me. But I'm very glad that you've shared this information, although 'glad' may be the wrong word. Until I know more, I have to be careful about treating Slocomb as a secret racist. But it looks as if he is."

"Let me tell you how Slocomb explained how he happened to have the poster. It's an interesting story, and I'm sure it's a lie." Henry proceeded to give the sheriff a detailed account of Slocomb's tale of how he had come into possession of the Nazi poster. "But it can't be true. The poster looks new, not like something of WW II vintage. I can't imagine what he's up to, but it scares me. I mean it makes it less likely that we'll ever see Martin again. Anybody who'd put up something like that and then lie about it just can't be trusted."

"Try to keep your spirits up, both of you," Carol said. "I agree that what you're telling me is bizarre, that Slocomb is almost certainly well outside the mainstream, and maybe dangerous. But we don't know what's become of your son. Okay? It's too soon to give up."

"I suppose so," Ruth said, speaking up for the first time since serving tea.

"Do you suppose you could bring some kind of action against Slocomb?" Henry was obviously more pessimistic than his wife."I'm not sure what I mean, but there must be some way to bring him to court."

"I'm going to see what I can do, but unless he's broken some law, he'll be able to claim freedom of speech. I intend to pay him another visit, however, and I'll be as tough as the law allows."

As Carol drove home after leaving the Kennedys, her mind was full of negative and very anxious thoughts about their son Martin. Why had a man who appeared to be a racist, even a Nazi sympathizer, hired a young and troubled African-American boy to be his handyman for the summer? A handyman he didn't really need. Her advice to keep spirits up seemed little more than a case of whistling in the wind. Any reservations about more actively pursuing the missing boy had quickly disappeared. She'd make another trip to the home of the hog owner on the hill. And she'd do it right now, even if it meant missing her glass of Chardonnay with Kevin.

CHAPTER 17

Adolph Slocomb stayed seated for close to ten minutes after the Kennedys left. Seated and worried. Then he got up, went to the bedroom, and hauled his suitcase out of the closet. The summer had been a difficult one for him, but he had managed to tough it out by using his head, by not panicking. Until today. Today he had made one serious error. He had failed to close the front door when he had gone to the hog shed. Normally it would not have mattered, because no one would have driven up his drive and gone onto the porch. But he should not have assumed that he would have no company. Rarely did he have company, but lately he had had too much company: a cyclist named Ernie Eakins, Ruth and Henry Kennedy, the sheriff of Cumberland County. The sheriff had actually paid him two visits. No, he had been careless when he should have been extra careful. This time there was no way he could correct his mistake after the fact. It was too late.

There was no need to take much with him. No need to conceal the fact he had lived here. Too many people knew, including, unfortunately, the sheriff. In any event, he wouldn't be coming back. So he'd get the hogs into the back of the big pickup truck, put the suitcase, a few business files, and something to eat on the seat beside him, and head out. In which direction? He'd decide that as he packed.

Unfortunately, this plan wasn't going to work. The problem was the hogs. There were too many of them. And they were too large. It took him only a few minutes to realize that putting six large and restless hogs in the back of the truck and transporting them to another place, a place he had yet to identify, was a task that he could not possibly accomplish quickly, if at all. The hogs would have to be butchered first. But it was the middle of summer, and most slaughtering normally takes place in the fall. To do it with even one or two hogs would take time; to do it with six would take hours, a whole day or more. If he did it anyway, would any of his regular customers buy the ribs, loin, or butt? Slocomb sat back down on the couch under the poster of Hitler and took a deep breath. He supposed that he could leave the hogs in their shed, but why waste all that money? Yet he realized that he had no choice, that he'd have to slaughter one to give himself some food for a week or two, and simply treat the other hogs as a loss. Otherwise, he'd almost certainly have to cope with the sheriff, and that he decided he could not do.

He went to the kitchen, took a beer from the fridge, and looked for something that would pass for supper. Adolph Slocomb was not the happiest man on the hilltop when he finished his meal and lay down on the couch. His watch told him that it was 8:48 when he was awakened by a loud rapping on the front door. He wasn't ready for any company, especially at this hour. He was least ready for Sheriff Kelleher, but there she was. She had obviously heard from the Kennedys about the Nazi poster, and she had not waited until the next morning to confront him about it.

Slocomb was hardly awake, but he knew he couldn't afford to talk with the sheriff in the groggy condition he was now in. He'd have to talk himself awake, steer clear of conversation about his plans, avoid walking into a trap, assuming she might lay one for him. He had no idea what that trap might be, but he had to be on his toes.

"What on earth are you doing here at this hour? Or should I say what are you doing here at all?"

"If you'll invite me in and let me have a seat, I'll tell you why I'm here. We need to talk, and this is as good a time as any. It's getting dark, so I'd suggest that you turn on a light or two."

Slocomb looked confused, unsure what he should do next. He wasn't used to taking orders from visitors. Until very recently, he hadn't been used to visitors.

"You want to talk about something right now? I'd rather we talk about whatever's on your mind tomorrow, even the day after. It's been a long day, and I'm tired. I was asleep when you knocked."

"I understand, but I've had a rather long drive and I'm in no position to put this off." Carol walked past the hog farmer and took a seat on the couch. "This is a comfortable spot. Why don't you sit over there," she said, gesturing to the opposite end of the couch, "or if you prefer, that chair appears to be vacant."

He started to protest the way she was taking over, but thought better of it and tried to be more amenable.

"You know that I like my privacy, sheriff. So I'm sure you aren't surprised that I'm not exactly thrilled that you decided to pay me a visit tonight. But I'm sure you think you have a good reason for being here, so I'd like to hear about it."

Carol smiled, and then turned around on the couch until she was facing the wall.

"Unlike some of your other visitors, I have never seen art on the wall behind the couch. Not until tonight, that is. It's quite a remarkable piece of work, isn't it? You've done me a favor, leaving it where I can finally see it. I really appreciate it."

She was sure her approach to the Nazi poster was annoying Slocomb, and perhaps she shouldn't be handling it that way. But he obviously knew why she was paying him this visit, and she doubted that she could make him feel better if she did it differently.

"I assume that the Kennedys have told you about the poster and said they were shocked by it. Is that the story?"

"That's right. They were particularly upset that their son, Martin, who was working for you, saw it every day and had to be disturbed by it."

"I find that hard to believe, sheriff. As you must know, Martin was a very retarded boy. I doubt that he knew anything about what was on the poster. It would have been simply a large picture to him. He may even have liked it."

"I wouldn't know about that. But Martin's parents were certainly disturbed. And, quite frankly, I was also shocked by what the Kennedys told me. We don't think very highly of the Nazis over here in the United States. Even the Germans deeply regret the fact that they embraced the Nazi movement in the thirties and forties. So what I want to know is why you hung a Nazi poster on your living room wall."

"As you know, having sat in this living room before, I rarely hung the poster here in my living room."

"Oh, please, Mr. Slocomb. Give me credit for some common sense. You typically had that poster on the wall when you didn't have company, and that was most of the time. When you had company, like me, you took it down to conceal the fact it was usually there on the wall. In other words, you liked the poster and kept it up when you could, but didn't want others to see it and assume that you were a Nazi sympathizer. Isn't that true?"

"Didn't the Kennedys tell you that I wasn't sympathetic to the Nazis? That I kept the poster because it was my uncle's memento of the war in which he fought."

"Yes, Mr. Kennedy told me that, but he didn't believe it. It was a poster turned out long after WW II, in much better shape than one from a church wall in the forties."

"Are you calling me a liar?"

"You may call what you are saying anything you like. But I'd much prefer that you tell me exactly why you have kept the poster and why you keep it up in your living room as often as you can. And why you hide it when you are afraid other people will see it. Look at it. It isn't a WW II trophy. It's too new, in too good shape. It didn't survive the war in your uncle's backpack. It was produced much more recently, probably by some company that caters to racists, to Nazis, right here in the United States. Why don't we take it off the wall and take a look at the back. I'll bet there's a label there, identifying the company from which you bought it. Come on, let's take a look."

"I think I've had enough of your accusations, and I'm going to ask you to leave."

"And I'm not leaving. Not yet, not until you tell me why you hired Martin Kennedy."

Slocomb got out of his seat and took a step toward the door. Then stopped.

"I hired him because I needed help. And I keep this poster on the wall because I have a constitutional right to free speech. If I want to say things you and the Kennedys don't like, that's my business. If I want to read *Mein Kampf*, I can read it and you have no right to tell me I can't. It happens that I've never read *Mein Kampf*, but that's because, unlike you smug intellectuals, I don't waste my time reading. Now that we've dealt with that issue, I'm going to insist that you get out of my house."

"In a minute or two, Mr. Slocomb. But first, if you're a racist, which you seem to be insisting that you are, why go to the trouble of hiding the poster when you have company? Why not let the world know what you are? Why not be proud of it? As you've said, our constitution protects free speech, even if that speech is rotten. And you really haven't answered my question as to why you hired the Kennedys' son. He knows nothing about hogs, and you've admitted that he's retarded, which would mean that he'd have a problem doing most kinds of handyman type of work. What do you have him doing?"

"He's missing, or had you forgotten. Now get out. I need my sleep."

Carol called it a night. She'd seen the poster, a disgusting piece of what could hardly be called art, and also seen Adolph Slocomb at his worst. But she still didn't know what Martin did while he worked there. She wasn't sure how she'd discover the answer to that question, but she knew that she was going to do whatever she had to do to find out.

CHAPTER 18

Unfortunately, her decision to pursue the question of what Slocomb had been doing with Martin had to be postponed, at least temporarily, because of developments in the matter of the other disappearance confronting the sheriff. It came via a phone call from Connie Eakins which interrupted Carol's breakfast with Kevin the next morning.

Connie had not been specific, but she had, as was her manner, sounded both worried and needful as she explained, or rather hinted, that her search for Ernie had taken another turn for which she needed the sheriff's help. Reluctantly Carol agreed to drop by the Eakins house that morning.

"What's the problem this time?" Kevin asked.

"It's Ernie Eakins's wife, and she's still trying to figure out why he never made it back from the Gravel Grinder. I'm afraid I agreed to see her as soon as I finish my breakfast."

"You're lucky you don't have more people dropping out of sight. But why go running up to the Eakins' place before you tackle the Kennedy's problem? Sounds to me as if what you learned about Slocomb is more important than the latest alarm from the cycling world."

"It probably is, but Mrs. Eakins gave me no details. Anyway, she sounded as if she's in panic mode again. Besides, if Slocomb is an honest to goodness neo-Nazi, he's not going to repent in a day or two. I know I'll get back to him soon, maybe even today."

Carol was to regret not insisting that Connie Eakins tell her more about why she needed to see her that morning. Had she done so, she might well have gotten back to Slocomb that day. As it was, she didn't see him nearly that soon.

But she did see Mrs. Eakins. The wife of the missing area cyclist was waiting for her on her porch when the sheriff arrived at 8:50.

"It's so good to see you sheriff," Connie said, although there was no enthusiasm in her greeting. "It's been another of those sleep-less nights. Do you ever have them?"

"I guess we all do, but I've been luckier than you have. My husband was right there this morning, just where he was supposed to be. But what about Ernie? Any word?

"No, none. But I may have a new idea. At least one that I didn't have a day ago. Come in and I'll tell you about it."

Carol was surprised, even cautiously hopeful. What did Connie mean by a new idea?

It was immediately apparent that Connie's new idea was not one that encouraged her. It had the effect of temporarily taking her mind off the belief that Ernie was dead. But what replaced that conviction was no better.

What had been responsible for planting a possibly new explanation for her husband's disappearance was an unexpected and unannounced visit from a woman she had heard of but never met, Valerie Leonard. She arrived on a bicycle, wearing scarlet shorts and top, her long blond hair under one of those helmets that serious cyclists always wear. When she introduced herself, Connie wasn't surprised to hear that she was finally meeting a woman she had heard Ernie mention more than once, a fellow bike rider. The reason for her visit was less obvious, and when she left the better part of an hour later Connie was still unsure what had prompted her to make the trip to the Eakins' home.

There had been the familiar expression of regret for having failed to come by and say hello earlier, and the apology for being so informally dressed (and so sweaty). But Valerie had spent most of her time in the Eakins' living room telling her how sorry she was about Ernie's disappearance and how hopeful she was that he would show up soon, hale and hearty as usual.

Initially, Connie had been grateful for a visit by a friend of her husband, a thoughtful attempt to cheer her up and wish her well. When she left, however, Connie felt somewhat differently about it. In the first place, Mrs. Leonard had never been her friend, but someone who frequently shared days in the countryside on county roads with Ernie. The more she thought about it, the more she began to imagine the two of them enjoying those outings, perhaps more than he enjoyed his own wife's company. It was but a short time before Mrs. Leonard became more than just a fellow cyclist; she became an attractive woman, a woman with shapely legs, a tight rear end, a charming smile and a head of hair that looked much lighter and more natural than her own. By the time she left, having once again wished her well, Connie was thinking of Valerie Leonard as a rival, and a rival with several pronounced advantages.

Like a lot of women, Connie had considered once or twice in the course of her married life whether her husband had an interest in other women, if not regularly at least occasionally. She typically ignored these fugitive thoughts and let her mind return to the comfortable feeling that she had a wonderful marriage. Ernie had never said anything which gave her a reason to be worried, nor had she ever seen him eyeing other women in a suspicious way. But what if he watched what he said and where he let his eyes wander, yet frequently carried on an affair with Mrs. Leonard in his mind. For all she knew, Ernie was sexually interested in Valerie. Maybe even in other women. Was it possible that he had disappeared during the Gravel Grinder because that interest had steered him off the path and into the arms of one of those other women?

Carol was astonished at the way Connie became increasingly committed to the 'other woman' explanation for Ernie's disappearance as she talked about Mrs. Leonard. She had even dug into Ernie's desk drawers and found a warm letter from a woman named Heaslip he had met at a bike race in the Dakotas.

"But Mrs. Eakins," Carol said to her when she paused in the course of her argument, "doesn't what you are saying seem unrealistic? I'm not denying that your husband may have an interest in another woman, although I hope that isn't the case and what you have told me certainly doesn't prove it. But it seems to me that using a long bike ride with over one hundred people to leave his wife is close to unbelievable. Excuse me for saying so, but if he really wanted to do it, wouldn't there be many other times and places that would make a lot more sense? And be much easier. Sorry, I shouldn't have said that. I think you are all worked up for no good reason, and you're not thinking clearly."

"You're probably right, but I can't help it. And I'm really worried about this Leonard woman. And the one from South Dakota."

"I'm sure you are. But you're making it harder for yourself. I'm not normally what you'd call an optimist, but my opinion is that Ernie is alive and not hiding somewhere with some other woman. What's more, I intend to talk with every member of the Gravel Grinder if I have to." The very thought of doing so promised to bring on a headache, but she no longer could see a way of finessing the task.

When she left the Eakins' residence, she knew that her day was going to be occupied with a visit to Valerie Leonard, assuming that she was available, plus planning conversations with other Gravel Grinders, an important mission which she had put off for too long already.

CHAPTER 19

Talking with the Gravel Grinders might as well begin with Mrs. Leonard. After all, she, too, was a Gravel Grinder, and one who was known to be friendly with Ernie Eakins. Then there would be visits to others who had been on the ride with Ernie the day he had disappeared. She'd already gotten their names from Joe Reiger. He had ticked off those on the list he'd given her that he knew to be Ernie's closest friends. She wasn't sure that this was the best way to proceed. Perhaps she should begin by seeing Ernie's 'enemies' first, but it took all of one minute to write off such a plan. It was highly unlikely that Joe would know if Ernie had enemies, or if so who they were. If he did, he would undoubtedly be reluctant to share their names; Joe would not wish to be seen as a gossip monger.

As it happened, Valerie Leonard was not out riding her bike. She was at home, apparently putting her house in shape after a night when her daughter had had a sleep over with several other girls. Mrs. Leonard sounded reluctant to have the sheriff see the house when it wasn't spic and span, but she agreed to do so. Carol made no reference to the fact that her visit was related to her conversation with Connie Eakins, only that she was in the process of talking with cyclists who had been on the Gravel Grinder with Ernie Eakins.

It was close to noon when Carol first met the woman who supposedly had shapely legs and a tight rear end. Not bad, she thought, but hardly the knock-out Connie had described.

"Like I told you over the phone," she said, "I'm officially investigating Ernie Eakins' disappearance, and that necessitates talking with his fellow bikers. Sorry to bother you, but I understand you know Ernie, ride with him frequently, might be able to help me."

"I know him, of course, but I don't know whether I'll be of much help. There were a lot of us on the ride last week, and I don't recall that Ernie and I rode together much of the way."

"Maybe you can tell me something about these bike trips. Do those on the trip stick together most of the way, sort of like a herd?"

"Oh goodness, no. It isn't a race, where you try to get a good lead and leave the others behind. We're a mixed group, different ages, different skills. It wouldn't be much fun if you had to stick together. I couldn't ride beside Johnny Warrener for very long. He must be 80, and he's no speedster, believe me. The purpose of the Gravel Grinder is to set your own pace, enjoy what you're doing."

"That's what I imagined," Carol said. "But on the ride you had recently did you and Ernie spend any of it near each other, close enough so you could talk, keep track of where you were, whether your bike was giving you any problems, that kind of thing."

"In other words, could I tell you if Ernie had to leave the trail we were on? Well, I'm afraid not. We were fairly close in the early going, but as time went on all of us spread out. So, frankly, I have no idea whether Ernie had a problem with his bike, took a break, anything like that. If he did and I knew about it, I'd have told Joe Reiger as soon as I got back to Southport."

"Did you hear anyone else on the ride mention Ernie, say he might have had a problem, what it was, where it happened?"

"I'm afraid not. If somebody did know something, he'd have told Joe. That's what's so weird about this. A good cyclist like Ernie, missing after a ride that was a workout but not all that demanding. It makes no sense."

"No it doesn't. I'm doing what I can to help his wife cope, but I'm as lost as she is."

Carol had had no reason to take seriously Connie Eakins' new explanation of her husband's disappearance. When she left the Leonard home, she was prepared to dismiss the idea entirely. For all she knew, Valerie and Ernie might have been more than friends, but she was sure that whatever had happened to him had nothing to do with the attractive cyclist.

Joe Reiger had been reluctant to suggest Gravel Grinders whom he would turn to first if he were trying to learn more about Ernie Eakins.

"I'm not talking about people who would be most likely to know what happened to him. I think we've pretty much exhausted that approach. I'm talking about people who know him best. His wife may know the answer to that question, but for some reason I doubt that she does. You've been watching our cyclists for years, and probably know as much as anyone about who's closest to him. In a biker sense, I mean."

"That's a tough one," Joe had said. "If you pushed me a bit, I might suggest one or two. I'd probably begin with Valerie Leonard."

"Interesting. I was talking with her just this morning, so I see we're on the same page."

"We are indeed." The look that had come over Joe's face suggested that he, like Connie Eakins, might have wondered whether there was more to the Leonard-Eakins friendship than cycling.

"Any others?" Carol asked.

"Perhaps." Joe paused, as if trying to come up with an appropriate reply. "How about Lester Gallagher? He and Ernie have been cycling pals for years. And then one more: Phil McCabe. He's more of a guess than Gallagher, but it would be a similar relationship. If you come up empty on those two, I'll see if I can smoke out someone else. How did you do with Leonard, by the way?"

"Not so well. We talked mostly about the Gravel Grinder, not about their friendship. But I'm still feeling my way. To be perfectly honest, I'm not optimistic about this investigation. It's not common for someone to go missing like Ernie has - goes biking with well over one hundred people and just vanishes like he did."

Now that she had shifted her attention from Martin Kennedy to Ernie Eakins, Carol realized that she would be visiting Gallagher and McCabe before she went back to Slocomb, much as she knew that the racist hog farmer interested her more.

Lester Gallagher was not available, so she tried McCabe. He was not only available, but more than ready to meet with the sheriff.

"I've been concerned about Ernie. I'm sure a lot of us are concerned. People just don't jump on their Hardtails and disappear like he did. I'd love to meet with you, but I can't promise to do more than share my worries with you."

"You know Ernie pretty well?"

"Yes and no. We aren't social friends, but we've been riding together for seven, eight years. Been on rides from Maine to Pennsylvania, could probably write a book on what not to do if you want to get some place and back in one piece."

They agreed to meet when Phil got home from work that day. Carol was surprised that McCabe didn't look like a great cyclist, not that she knew how to judge who was a great cyclist. But he didn't look like he weighed more than 140 pounds, and neither his arms or legs were as muscular as she expected those of a serious bike rider to be.

"Thanks for taking the time for this," she said as they took seats on the lakeside deck and his wife brought them ice tea. "I didn't know Mr. Eakins - may I call him Ernie? - before his wife sought my help in finding out what happened to him. But his disappearance is really a puzzle. This probably isn't the way to start our discussion, but do you have a guess, a hunch, as to the answer to the problem?"

"I wish I did, but the answer is no. I don't remember seeing him after the first mile or two."

"Okay. You say you've ridden with him a fair number of times. Forgetting races, can you tell me anything about the way he usually tackles an event like this one? Does he take it easy, stay in the back of the pack? Or does he step on the gas - you know what I mean, instinctively move to the front?"

"He's a good rider, meaning he quite naturally doesn't hang back. He'd find that boring, But neither is he a show off, someone who likes to treat every event as a race, something he wants to win. There've been events where he and I stick together most of the time, talk about things. And times when he seems to enjoy being by himself. You a cyclist? If so, you can probably imagine how it is, your mood different from one time to another."

"No, I'm afraid I haven't done much riding since I was a kid. Nor is my husband a cyclist. I don't have much experience to go on."

"Let's talk about the Gravel Grinder. This one, where Ernie went missing. Think about it. Were there places where it would have been easy to miss a turn, get lost? Joe Reiger drove me around the whole route, but I was just getting a feel for it all, not possible trouble spots."

"I'm not sure. Ernie knows this area pretty well, so it's unlikely." McCabe closed his eyes, as if to think harder. After a few seconds, he shook his head, opened his eyes. "Maybe there's one place, but I have no idea whether it would be a challenge for Ernie. It wasn't for me, but that's not what we're talking about and we can't ask Ernie."

"Tell me about it."

"Unless you know the county quite well - excuse me, sheriff, you probably know it better than I do -" McCabe looked embarrassed. "Anyway, it's a hard place to describe, but let me try. It's on a back road that eventually takes you to Watkins. A place where the Gravel Grinder turned left, north. One could keep going straight, miss the turn. But I'm pretty sure Ernie would have realized his mistake after a mile or two and turned around, so that doesn't sound very promising. Besides, somebody else would presumably have seen him, called out to turn back."

Carol had briefly considered this possibility when she was covering the Gravel Grinder route with Joe Reiger, but the case was then too new and her knowledge of it too limited. But as she processed Phil's thought, it occurred to her that she knew, more or less, where he had in mind. And it was a place where she had been very recently, and not just once.

CHAPTER 20

By the end of the day, Carol had come, however tentatively, to two conclusions. Two conclusions that might tie two different problems together. The first was that Adolph Slocomb was almost certainly a racist. The second was that Ernie Eakins had probably gone off the Gravel Grinder route somewhere in the vicinity of Slocomb's house. That Slocomb was probably a racist, even a latter day Nazi, was considerably more likely than that Eakins had wandered off the track near where Slocomb lived. After all, she had seen the poster with Hitler and a swastika, but she hadn't talked with anyone who had been riding with Ernie near Slocomb's. Moreover, the hog farmer had claimed not to have seen the cyclist, and his response to her question about it had seemed to be convincing.

But was it possible that Slocomb had lied, that Eakins had indeed been on his property, that he had seen him, even talked to him, and that Ernie being missing had something to do with that encounter? It was too soon, much too soon, for her to blame what had happened to Eakins on Slocomb, just as it was too soon to blame Martin Kennedy's disappearance on him. Nonetheless, the more she thought about it the more she found herself wondering whether Eakins' disappearance and Kennedy's disappearance might somehow be related. They had taken place at about the same time, and they might have taken place at or very close to the same location on a sparsely inhabited hill east of Crooked Lake. Yet what could a missing white cyclist have to do with a missing young and retarded black boy?

Carol was in Southport, on her way home, when it occurred to her that she might as well try Gallagher again. His number and address were back at the office, but she was within a block of the

Chamber of Commerce building and Joe Reiger, and could get the necessary information from him. Fortunately there was a parking space available, so she took advantage of it.

"Hi, Joe. Just dropped by to get Lester Gallagher's address, again. Thought I'd pay him a visit on my way home."

"Not today," spoke up Jean Lewis from her chair at the receptionist's desk. "He's out of town until the weekend, according to his wife."

"Not true," Joe said. "I saw him in the post office this morning. If you're going to keep our community up to date on who's where, Jean, you need to get your facts straight."

"Oh, sorry about that. Sallie should have known better."

Carol got the number and address, called the Gallagher residence, and, learning that Lester was at home, headed for the Gallagher's.

She didn't expect to learn anything new or helpful, but she was saving another trip down to Southport.

"Glad to catch you at home," she said as she shook hands and took a seat on the living room couch. "I won't be long, but I'm doing my best to track down Ernie Eakins, and Joe Reiger said you might be helpful."

"Ernie? What's his problem?"

"That's what we don't know. But you were on the Gravel Grinder with him last week, so I thought I'd ask you a few questions, see if you might help me find him."

"Sorry to be confused, but I don't know what this is about. You can't find Ernie? Did you ask his wife?"

"It sounds as if you must have left town right after the Gravel Grinder. I've assumed everyone knew about this, but I guess I'm wrong. The problem is that Ernie never showed up back here in the village after your bike ride. What did you do when you finished it?"

"You're telling me that Ernie's gone missing? He didn't tell his wife where he'd gone? I'll be damned. That's strange, doesn't sound like Ernie. But no, I heard nothing about this. Headed for home almost as soon as I crossed the finish line because I'd promised Jim Tyler I'd meet him down in Lewisburg. We had some business we had to straighten out for the Tri-State Company. But that's irrelevant; you aren't interested in Tri-State. And you're saying that Ernie's disappeared for - what is it - almost a week? That's unbelievable. I've never known him to pull something like that. Connie doesn't know where he is? None of the other people who were on the ride? What about Reiger, Ernie's family? I think he's got a cousin who lives in Sayre. They been called?"

It was obvious that Lester Gallagher was genuinely puzzled by this news. And really worried.

"I'm as buffaloed as you are, Mr. Gallagher. As you can imagine, his wife is beside herself. I've been working on this for days, made no progress. Let's try a little brainstorming. You know Eakins much better than I do. What his interests are, who he hangs out with, what he does, other than cycles whenever he has a chance."

"What do you think I can do to help?"

"For example, what do you know about Ernie's marriage? As far as you know, is his relationship with Connie solid?"

Gallagher was surprised by the question. His face darkened.

"What are you getting at? Has something come up that suggests his disappearance is related to marital problems? That sounds pretty far fetched."

Carol didn't want to discuss Connie's comments about Valerie Leonard, but simply open the door to the possibility that Ernie might have a wandering eye.

"It probably is far fetched, but I have to consider any possible explanation for what's happened to him."

"That I understand, but I can't imagine that Ernie just took off somewhere on something like the Gravel Grinder to have a roll in the hay with some babe. It would be hard to do without someone noticing. More importantly, Ernie's a straight shooter, as far as I know. My wife and I aren't exactly close to the Eakins, but I've never heard anything that suggests that his marriage to Connie is in trouble. Has someone told you it is?"

Was this the time to create an even deeper hole for poor Connie? Probably not.

"No. You know how it is, people start speculating when something strange like this happens. So no, only off the wall guesswork."

"Glad to hear it. I'd forget it if I were you."

"Do you think you might be able to help find Ernie? Not join my investigation, nothing like that. But think about it - about Ernie - and maybe something will occur to you that could help me. And Connie. Something that may or may not be important, but has slipped out of your mind today. Something you saw or heard when you were riding with him and all those other guys - and women - last week. Nothing may come to you, but it's been my experience that things that seem irrelevant sometimes become more important on reflection."

"Well sure, but I'd be kidding you and myself if I thought I'd have a brainstorm."

"I know what the odds are, but I appreciate it that you'd try. Thanks." Carol had deliberately ignored the possibility that Ernie Eakins was dead. Perhaps Lester would come to that possibility himself, and even have an idea as to why and where.

CHAPTER 21

As she was driving home, Carol passed a roadside stand that looked as if it might have something to supplement what Kevin was doing for dinner. She pulled off on the shoulder and was about to step out of the car when a large pickup truck roared past her. She was annoyed by its speed, and reflexively tried to make a mental note of its license number. No luck. But the truck itself looked familiar. It was while she was tucking several ripe tomatoes and a raspberry pie into the back seat that she remembered where she had seen it. It had been parked by the shed behind Adolph Slocomb's house. Where was he going at such breakneck speed?

This in turn reminded her that she had set aside her issues with Slocomb while she dealt once again with the Eakins case. She would get back to Slocomb tomorrow, now with one more complaint, speeding. But it wasn't to give him a ticket that she'd revisit him. It was to have a more serious discussion with him about why he had hired Martin Kennedy, a decision that never made much sense and now seemed even more reprehensible due to the fact that the boy had been subjected to the Nazi poster on a daily basis.

Carol considered Slocomb the rest of the way back to the cottage. She even considered the thought that McCabe had planted in her mind without knowing he had done so: that not only the Kennedy case, but possibly the Eakins case as well, might have involved Slocomb.

"Here," she called out to Kevin, "I thought I'd ease my conscience with some goodies for dinner. The tomato season is really here, and it's always the season for raspberry pies."

"Great ideas, both of them. But let's take the canoe out before I serve up. You up to it?"

"Of course, as long as you don't criticize me for not finding young Kennedy. Or Ernie Eakins. I also failed to catch Slocomb speeding down the East Lake Road as well."

"Bad day, I take it. I promise not to rub it in. Mine was pretty ordinary, too."

"Tell you what. Let's not discuss our bad day, yours and mine. Only positive things."

"What positive things do you have in mind?"

"Be creative. Another cruise, a trip to Key West or maybe the Maritime Provinces. Be sure to include good weather."

In a few minutes they had pushed the canoe into the lake and headed south toward Mallard Point. For awhile they didn't talk at all, enjoying the quiet pleasure of dipping their paddles into the water while the sun sank slowly over the vineyards on the hills to their west.

Kevin broke the silence.

"What's this about not catching the speeding Slocomb?"

"I thought we weren't going to talk about the bad news."

"I forgot," Kevin said. "Anyway, lake speeders aren't really bad news, not like missing cyclists and handymen. Especially when the guy who's speeding is a Nazi sympathizer. Maybe he'll crash his car and end up in the hospital for a month or two."

"Or take out another car and put several people in the hospital. Besides, Slocomb is, without a question, more of my bad news. I've got to pay him another visit tomorrow, try to find out why he had to hire the Kennedy boy. Imagine, a racist who chooses an African-American kid to help him."

"Maybe he was trying to mend his ways, prove that he's a new man."

"You should meet him, listen to him. He's no new man."

Their agreement not to talk about the sheriff's cases having been broken, the conversation quickly settled into Carol's effort to bring Kevin up to date on her problems.

"I take no pleasure out of being a pessimist," she said. "But when people disappear without a clue as to where they went, and then stay disappeared for a week, you've got to begin to think the worst."

"Meaning, you're beginning to suspect that both Eakins and Kennedy are dead?"

"What would you think?"

Kevin left his paddle in the water. The canoe drifted slowly past the last cottage on the point.

"I might agree. But you tend to suspect coincidences, and you're left with a really unusual one. A cyclist who rides well, has ridden the back roads for years, is suddenly dead on a challenging but hardly a difficult ride. And the same day, or close to it, a young retarded boy who's got an easy job also drops dead. Neither case makes much sense, yet there they are, two unaccountable deaths on Crooked Lake, back to back. And neither one with a clue as to what happened or where the bodies are. You're the coincidence avoider. How do you explain it?"

"I can't, not yet. I keep hoping that they'll show up, or that I'll get a phone call that says at least one of them has been accounted for. But nothing's happened, and time's passing. You see why I wanted not to talk about the bad days?"

"Of course I do," Kevin said. "And maybe you'll solve one of the problems tomorrow. Or rather Slocomb will solve it for you."

Carol didn't say anything. But she was sure that Slocomb wouldn't be of any help.

CHAPTER 22

Carol finished her breakfast, downed what was left of a second cup of coffee, and gave Kevin a hurried kiss before setting off for the Slocomb residence on the east lake hill. The racist hog farmer hadn't answered his phone, but she wasn't concerned that he hadn't. Given the mood he was in when last she saw him, she was sure she would have the advantage if she surprised him.

The possibility that he would be in bed crossed her mind as she passed through Southport. But even if he were, the advantage would still be hers, and it would be even stronger. Her distaste for the man cancelled any feeling that waking him up would be rude or impolite. But she knew he would be up, probably out in the shed feeding his hogs.

The road to the deteriorating house had no traffic once she got out of Southport. A night time thunder storm had left much of the road wet with occasional pools of water, and once she reached the turn to Slocomb's abode the pools turned to mud. Why would anyone, even a racist and an unpleasant grouch, want to spend his days in such a wretched place?

It was immediately apparent that Slocomb wasn't at home. At least his pickup truck, last seen speeding down the East Lake Road, was nowhere in sight. He must have gone to town, Carol thought, although he had told her more than once that he much preferred to hunker down in his remote hilltop home. She parked by the shed and walked carefully through the mud to the front porch.

Her knocks on the front door went unanswered for more than a minute, reinforcing her initial impression that Slocomb was indeed not at home. Rather than return to the car and head for the department office in Cumberland, she pushed on the door to confirm that he was not there. To her surprise, the door slowly swung open. She debated going on in, then decided she had better do so. Perhaps something had happened to Slocomb, although the absence of the pickup truck told her that this was unlikely. She smelled coffee, and then an even stronger and less pleasant odor, also from the kitchen.

"Mr. Slocomb, are you here?" There was no answer, but she was sure that there wouldn't be. With no sunlight coming through the windows, the living room was fairly dark, but not so dark that she couldn't see that the Nazi poster had been removed from the wall.

Carol had never been in any other room of the house, but it was time to change that. The kitchen was first. As expected, the coffee pot was still warm. What was unexpected was on the kitchen table - chunks of meat, obviously recently cut from what was left from two hog carcasses lying on the floor, still slippery from their blood. She knew very little about such things, but enough to realize that the meat was inedible waste. Slocomb must have slaughtered the hogs right there in the kitchen and taken the edible cuts to shops in town early that morning. But why had he left the kitchen in such a mess? She would have cleaned it up before leaving. No, she said to herself, she would not have killed and carved up the hogs on the kitchen table where he presumably ate his meals. Carol had a momentary feeling that she might be going to throw up.

For all she knew, Slocomb might return at any minute. Better to complete her search of the house and go back to the car to wait for him.

There wasn't much more to the house. A small bedroom, a cluttered and dirty bathroom, and an L-shaped room with a desk, a chair, and a file, open and almost empty. The bed was unmade, the bedside lamp still turned on. On the wall over the bed was the only 'work of art' in the house other than the Nazi poster. It was a Confederate flag which, unlike the poster, was unmounted and unframed. It was also peeling away from the wall on the corner nearest to the bedside lamp. Adolph Slocomb lived in a veritable rat's nest.

Carol wanted to examine the rat's nest more carefully, but she didn't want to have Slocomb find her doing so. She had no idea when he would be back, but guessed that mid- to late morning was most likely. Much as she hated doing it, she went back to the car. Finding no reading material there, she turned on the radio and settled in for a boring but necessary wait for the owner.

A combination of Golden Oldies and breaking news did nothing to perk her up, and by 10:30 Carol was as frustrated as she could remember being in many months. Slocomb had not returned, and her expectation that he would had now largely disappeared. Was he to be the third person on the hill above Crooked Lake to vanish in less than two weeks?

She shifted her attention from the uninspiring radio to thoughts as to what she might do rather than kill time in her car behind the hog shed. Two things occurred to her, neither one for the first time. She might drive over to Slocomb's neighbor, Lew Guernsey, and see if he might have seen either Martin Kennedy or Ernie Eakins. Having heard Slocomb's views regarding his neighbor and checked out the distance to his house, Carol had written him off some time ago. But doing so may have been too hasty. The other idea focussed on the ravine. It was also a considerable distance from Slocomb's, but, more importantly, it was, at this point high above the lake, very steep, the bottom way below and well out of sight. She knew she should have searched it, but she was aware that doing so would be dangerous. Better to pursue other leads, exhaust other options first. Unfortunately, there had been no other promising leads, only more conversations with Slocomb, Connie Eakins, Henry and Ruth Kennedy, and a few of Ernie's fellow riders.

As the morning went by, the ravine gradually became the better option. She had already, nearly a week earlier, walked to it, and discovered how large and inaccessible it was. What is more, she had been unable to see anyone who might have fallen and landed on a ledge or in a tree. There was no way she could or should tackle the ravine by herself. It was a job for some of her officers, and a challenging one that even her toughest, younger men would recognize as hazardous. But it would have to be done, and perhaps it night lead to catching a glimpse of Eakins or Kennedy, or, if not either of them, perhaps Ernie's bicycle.

These thoughts did not, however, rescue her from a wasted morning. It was now almost noon, and she had either to go back to the office or risk having Slocomb, later than she had imagined, catch her snooping around in his house. She decided to take her chances on Slocomb.

Reasonably confident that she would have the house to herself, Carol headed for the room with the desk and the file. The file was open and contained only a few papers, but it was most likely of anything she saw in the house to contain something of importance. The papers were mostly sales slips regarding meat from the hogs. She made no attempt to keep these papers, but she did copy on one of them the names of the the stores where Slocomb did business. It was only as she folded this paper to stuff into her jacket pocket that she noticed that on the back it contained a scribbled, barely legible reference to a place called North Forester. The name meant nothing to Carol, but the paper stayed in her pocket because it also contained the names of the Crooked Lake stores where he sold his meat. Not that she expected to learn much by doing so, but she planned to speak to the managers of all the stores on the list.

Carol went through all of the rooms, but found nothing else of interest. There was still the hog pen, but while the hogs Slocomb had not cut up in the kitchen might still be there, they would of course be unable to tell her anything.

It was close to two when she decided to give up on seeing Slocomb. She had had no chance to question him as to why he had found it necessary to hire Martin Kennedy, but she now had a new question. Where had he gone? And when would he be back?

CHAPTER 23

"This may seem like a silly question, but have any of you spent time in the ravines here on the lake? Not getting your feet wet, but doing some serious climbing." It was the way Carol opened the next morning's squad meeting the next morning, and it produced a few smiles and three raised hands.

Parsons lowered his hand but spoke up.

"I don't know what you have in mind, but I'll confess. It was my favorite outdoor sport when I was a kid. Got a few skinned knees and I can't remember how many 'be carefuls' from my mother. But that was years ago. My sciatica keeps me out of the ravines these days. What's going on?"

"We need to search a ravine on the east lake road. It's related to that missing cyclist and the African-American kid who disappeared last week. You've all been pretty much uninvolved in this one. It hasn't seemed like something our department needed to worry about, but you know me and now I have a hunch we need to step in. At least to the extent of searching this ravine."

"So you're looking for ravine climbers?" Officer Damoth asked. "Well, count me in. It's the way I keep in shape, sort of."

"Me, too," added Officer Dockery. "Mom thinks I go up the ravines to hang out with boys, so it'll be nice to tell her it's part of my job."

Carol had told herself when she hired Dockery that the young woman would have the same assignments as the men. But she knew she didn't want her scrambling up - or down - the big ravine next to Slocomb's place. Explaining this to her youngest and smallest officer would be a test of her management skills. She'd leave it until after the squad meeting.

"Anyone else?"

It turned out that five wanted to join what sounded like an adventure. She thought that three would be enough, four if she counted herself as crew leader inasmuch as she knew where they would be going and what they would be looking for.

At least the weather had settled down, reducing the problem of a slippery bank. And Dockery had been given another assignment; she probably realized that the boss didn't want her in the ravine, but she reluctantly chose not to make an issue of it.

Carol told the ravine team to be back at headquarters by 11:00, unless she changed her instructions, and she set off for Slocomb's to see if she needed to do so. But as she expected, there was no evidence that he had returned to what she was thinking of as the rat's nest. The smell of coffee had disappeared, the smell left by the slaughtered hogs was worse, the Nazi poster was still missing, and nothing had been done to neaten the house. Time to tackle the ravine.

It made more sense to work down from the plot next to Slocomb's than to drive down to the bottom of the ravine and work up. If either Kennedy or Eakins was in the ravine, it would certainly be because he had fallen in from above, and there were many places where his body might be lodged well before it reached the floor of the ravine. So Carol parked where the drive to the Slocomb house left the hill top road, and waited for her colleagues to follow her map and arrive with the equipment which would make the exploration of the ravine as safe as possible.

While she waited, she thought about what they might find. She doubted that they'd find Eakins, an experienced adult who knew the lake well and had probably spent as much time in its ravines as had her search party. Kennedy was another story, both because of his youth, his unfamiliarity with the lake, and, of course, his re-

tarded condition. But she had been told that he was not a wan-
derer, that he stayed near home, and in this case that meant Slocomb's house.

But what if either or both of them were pushed or thrown
into the ravine? Just a day or two earlier Carol would have dismissed this possibility. Slocomb was an unpleasant man, but he
had claimed that he had never seen Eakins or even knew who he
was and that Kennedy had disappeared while he had been in town
taking care of business. There had been no reason to doubt his
word. And then had come the discovery of the Nazi poster. Assuming that it branded Slocomb as a racist, it didn't prove that
he had had anything to do with the death of Martin or Ernie. But
she couldn't shake the suspicion that it might have. The fact that
he had vanished so soon after the poster had come to light only
heightened that suspicion. Why else had he disappeared? Because
others, one of them a sheriff, now believed he was a racist? Unlikely. Most racists liked to flaunt their views on the subject. Many
ranted on talk radio. Some sought to influence American politics.
All of them knew that the first amendment to the constitution de-
fended these rights.

Her map proved to be acceptable, and her officers came to a
stop on the dirt road to Slocomb's house, looking eager to tackle
the ravine.

"The owner's not here?" It was Officer Damoth's question.

"Seems not," Carol said. "Trouble is, he's disappeared, which is
why no one's here to greet us. Anyway, our job is over there." She
pointed to the ravine, some distance away toward the crest of the
hill to their south.

"It looks like we should be able to drive over to it and park," said
Deputy Sheriff Bridges, who had insisted that he should be a part
of the climbing team.

It was not until they stood on the bank above the ravine that
Carol and the others realized how difficult a task they faced. Lay-
ing below them were the tops of a great many trees and bushes,

so thick and numerous that from where they stood the rock wall of the ravine was hard to see. Which meant that rappelling down it would be difficult.

"I'm not so sure that my plan is as good as I thought it would be," Carol said. "Which means that we may have to drive down to the lower road and that we've wasted quite a bit of time." She felt somewhat foolish.

"Maybe not," Sam said. "It may be easier if we move around to the other side. The foliage doesn't look so dense over there."

"True," Carol agreed, "but if Kennedy or Eakins fell into the ravine, why would they go all the way to the south side to do it. It makes no sense." Maybe the whole thing made no sense. No matter what they did, exploring the ravine was going to be a tough job and a dangerous one. She had been too sure that if either Martin or Ernie were down there, their bodies would probably be seen from the ridge on which they were standing. And from where they were standing, no bodies could be seen.

"Tell you what." It was Sam, trying to help his boss out. "Why don't I get suited up and make my way down the bank. Not all the way, but far enough that I should be able to see if there's a body in all those trees."

"No, let me do it." It was Officer Damoth. "You've got quite a few years on me, so it's my job."

Sam chose not to argue the matter.

It took a while to get ready for the descent, and then Damoth set off, cautiously, hugging the bank as well as he could and shouting his progress as he made his way down through the dense foliage. They had heard nothing from him that mentioned sighting any bodies when Sam felt the rope slide suddenly through his hands and heard Damoth holler something that was unintelligible but made it clear that he was in trouble.

It was an hour and forty minutes later that a rescue truck and crew, with some assistance from Carol's team, got to Damoth and brought him to the surface of the ravine. He was suffering from a broken arm, the result of his effort to stop a fall. He was obviously in pain, but was doing his best to treat it as a minor problem, one that he had incurred while performing the duties he had committed himself to when he agreed to join the Cumberland County sheriff's department. Carol was worried about him and what she had in effect asked him to do. His other colleagues also expressed their concern, but spent much of the time kidding him when it became apparent that his 'wounds' were not that serious.

Carol chose not to continue the search for Kennedy and Eakins, at least not that afternoon. Perhaps Slocomb would come back, in which case she would change tactics and threaten him if he didn't tell her the truth about the two disappearances. If he didn't reappear, she'd think of some other way to pursue the possibility that there was indeed a body in the ravine. She decided not to share with her officers her conviction that she had handled the ravine exercise badly. They might agree with her, but it was more likely that they would regard Damoth's fall as mere bad luck and regret that their mission had not been a success.

She'd save her self-criticism for Kevin, who undoubtedly would tell her that Damoth's fall was not her fault. In any event, the more important problem was that she still did not know where Martin Kennedy and Ernie Eakins were. Or whether she had also lost Adolph Slocomb. He might be back at the hog farm some day soon, but Carol was increasingly of the opinion that she had seen the last of him.

CHAPTER 24

Adolph Slocomb's unkempt truck was rolling down route 15 in northern Pennsylvania. The traffic was light, as it almost always was. The scenery was impressive, with forested hills on all sides. But Slocomb was not interested in the scenery or the fact that villages were few and far between, creating long distances between places where it was possible to use a restroom. Eventually he would be in Williamsport, and he had no interest in spending much time in Williamsport. The truth of the matter was that he had no idea where he was going, what town or village would become his next home now that he had left Southport, New York. He had considered the subject off and on ever since he had packed the cuts of pork in a modest sized freezer, put it on the floor of the passenger side, and left the hilltop house without closing, much less locking, the door. Now approximately 75 miles from what had been home for two years, he was still having trouble deciding where would be a good - and safe - place to live. For that matter, what would he do once he got there? Not hog farming. The initial costs would be too great. He spat out an oath, expressing his irritation that he had had to leave a pen full of hogs behind. Somebody unknown would assume responsibility for them, unless they had died in the interim for lack of food.

He had considered in a half-hearted way which direction he should take. He knew it would be unwise to stay in the Finger Lakes region, where he surely had a reputation of sorts. For a brief time he thought about heading north into the Adirondacks, but decided it would only turn out to be an even less well populated version of the Finger Lakes, and while he wanted a small town, largely rural area, northern New York would surely take him even further from where he could expect to find organized white supremacist groups. Well, maybe it wouldn't, but if it did he would have wasted time and distance. In fact, that is what he had been doing ever since he had left Virginia. Why had he been such a fool?

Of course he had had no choice. He couldn't stay longer in Virginia, much less in the conservative hinterland of the state's southern or northwestern regions. It was there that he had participated in his last white supremacist demonstration, an event that had given him the pleasure that always came when he joined like-minded believers and challenged what he thought of as the multitudes who accepted a multi-cultural society. Unfortunately, there had been a skirmish at the demonstration. The press had called it a 'racial war' or worse, blaming the white supremacists as the left wing media always did for what had happened. And what had happened included a casualty. One of the counter-demonstrators had been seriously hurt and become a news-worthy coma patient in a local hospital. Adolph would still be living in Virginia had it not been for the fact that some bystander had photographed one of the white supremacists slamming the head of one of the liberal multi-culturalists on the pavement. And he had been the one caught on camera. Less than a week later he had disappeared into the no-man's land of western New York, bearing a hastily adopted new name, scruffier clothes, and a lot more facial hair.

Now, having abandoned the idea of going to the Adirondacks, he was driving south and getting closer to Williamsport. The drive had given Adolph a chance to review what he had been doing and what had been its consequences. While he would have liked to maintain relationships with other white supremacists and neo-Nazis, and to give his white rage the outlet of street demonstrations, he knew that because of that damned photographer he had to lay low. It had not been easy. Among other things, it had made him a recluse, largely confined to his musty home. And while most of the people he had gotten to know were politically conservative, they seemed to lack his intense dislike for African-Americans, Hispanics, and other interlopers in white America. Perhaps this was because people from other cultures were only a small minority of the Crooked Lake population and hence no apparent threat to most local lives and values.

But he had always thrived on aggression, a need to challenge those with whom he disagreed, and the opportunity to do so had been at least temporarily taken away by what had happened in Virginia. And that had led to a decision that he was responsible for but that he now found himself regretting.

He knew of only a handful of African-American families on or around Crooked Lake (why had he gotten in the habit of using that politically correct name when he had always referred to them as 'niggers?'). Normally he would have avoided them. But one of these families, he had been told, had a badly retarded teenage son, and the fact gave him a strange but interesting idea. What if he were to hire the boy and pay him enough attention that he would come to do what he demanded. He would not do it because he and the boy had, in an unexpected way, bonded. Far from it. He would do it because the boy would have become his slave, subject to his control. Initially he rejected the idea; it was so far from anything he had ever done, or even thought of doing. But he had never quite been able to put it out of his mind, and after all he believed that he was superior to African-Americans who never deserved the status they had gained from a weak government that had betrayed its white citizens. So eventually he visited the boy's parents, maintaining an approach which was thoroughly dishonest but ultimately successful. Unfortunately, his plan never came to fruition because the boy only remained in his employ for less than a week. That, of course, was another story.

Adolph didn't want to revisit Martin Kennedy's 'disappearance' at the moment, so he turned on the truck radio and found a channel which was playing folk music of the Vietnam War era. Within half an hour he was in South Williamsport, looking for one of the motels which catered to the crowds attending the Little League World Series. He knew there wouldn't be one which had an oven or microwave to cook some of the pork in his small freezer, but the pork cuts would last until he found a new home. The new home would probably not be located in the Williamsport area. He was there only because he had opted to drive south when he left Southport, and he had done that for no specific reason. It was the other direction from the Adirondacks and his immediate task was simply to get away from Crooked Lake. He had no idea where he would next pitch camp, only that it would not be in Virginia, where the cops were looking for him, or in the Finger Lakes, where they soon might be doing so. Ideally, it would be in an area where white supremacists like himself were fairly numerous and hopefully well organized. That had not been the case on Crooked Lake, in spite of the rumors to the contrary which had taken him there.

He pulled into the parking lot of a seedy motel and took out his wallet. It was heavy because it contained three folders he always carried with him. They weren't labeled, but he knew exactly what was in them. He set aside the one with information about Michael Decker, his real name, then opened the one with data about Adolph Slocomb. That was the name he had used when he left Virginia, when he could no longer identify himself as Michael Decker. Slocomb had come from a cousin, Adolph from a decision to honor the German dictator. He was no longer as sure as he had once been that Adolph had been a good choice, much as he had been proud to call himself that. In any event, he would no longer be able to use the given name and surname he had gone by during his time at Crooked Lake. So he opened the third folder, and found himself reading about someone named Kenneth Clemens.

He couldn't remember why he had chosen that name, but now it would be his, beginning when he signed in at the motel. Like the others, the Clemens folder was old and wrinkled. It dated back to when he had been in his early twenties and first realized that he might need to have identities other than Decker if he were occasionally going to supplement his income outside of the law. He had spent several days putting together everything he thought he would need if he were to assume another name, but it wasn't until what happened at the protest march in Virginia that it became necessary to use the information in a non-Decker folder. Initially he worried that becoming Slocomb wouldn't work, but to his surprise it had. Now he would have to become Clemens. He returned the now useless folders on Decker and Slocomb to his wallet, climbed out of his truck, and walked into the motel.

The desk clerk had been surprised that he was going to pay cash, but he didn't yet have his Clemens' credit card and agreeably offered to pay for the night in exchange for the room key. Traveling with his third name in less than three years was going to be challenging, but he had coped with similar problems as Slocomb and was confident that he could do it again.

When he finally got to his room, he found that it was both undistinguished and much better than the one he had left above Crooked Lake. He kicked off his boots and sprawled on the bed, where he tried a few TV stations before settling for one where a reporter was foolishly standing on a street corner in a town he'd never heard of, covering a tornado. He was in a foul mood, and found himself wishing that the town on the screen would be demolished.

Apparently the tornado missed the town, for an ad came on shortly. Adolph/Kenneth let his mind return to the failure of his effort to make Martin Kennedy his semi-slave. It no longer made any difference, and thinking about it only made him more annoyed. The boy would never become anybody's part time slave because he was now dead. He knew this because he had killed him. He hadn't wanted to because there had still been a possibility that the slave strategy might work out. But he had had no choice.

He remembered the day when it happened, and it was all because a man on a bicycle had ridden up to the house to explain that he had a problem and needed some help. All he needed, he recalled, was for me to fill his water bottle; that it was empty was his fault, not mine. But there he was, cycling on dirt roads and on someone else's property. He acted as if I should help him; apparently cyclists were in the habit of helping each other. But I'm no cyclist, and I wanted him to leave. And he wouldn't, not until I filled his bottle. So we stood there arguing on the porch where I was sitting, eating a peach pie, when the Kennedy boy came out the front door, wearing only his undershorts and acting worried about his clothes.

I thought the cyclist would use Martin's arrival to get off my porch. But of course he didn't. He stopped talking about his bicycle and began to ask me about the boy. And stupid Martin made things worse by taking off his shorts to tell me what his problem was. There I was with a dumb black mongoloid kid, almost naked. The cyclist lost his interest in his bike and began to ask me what was going on. It only took about a minute before he was accusing me of heaven knows what - I wasn't sure what he thought I was doing, but it was obvious that he didn't like the look of things. Then he said he was going to talk to the local government about it.

I lost my temper, and why not? Here was a stranger, on my property, taking my time and then threatening to go to the authorities with a complaint. What was I to do? I couldn't let him do that. So I grabbed an old snow shovel that had been sitting there since the previous winter and hit him over the head. He went down and I kept on smacking him until he stopped breathing. Problem solved, except that the boy had seen it all. I had to kill him, too. He might be dumb, but he'd be sure to tell his parents what he'd seen and I'd be in real trouble.

And then what? The answer came to me right away. Dump him in the ravine and tell his parents that he'd wandered off. If his body was found, everyone would assume he'd fallen into that big hole. Neat, I thought. Of course the cyclist had to be taken care of, too, but two bodies in the ravine was one too many. It took time to solve that problem - nearly three hours actually - but it had been well taken care of early afternoon.

All of this was old news by now, and while the sheriff of Cumberland County might find the Kennedy boy's body, she would have no reason to believe that his fall had not been an accident and she would never find the cyclist's body. Moreover, and more important, she will never find me either. All I have to do is find another place, far from Crooked Lake, to live, with a new name and a past that she knows nothing about. She may think I am a Nazi sympathizer, but so what? She will never be able to link the Hitler-Swastika poster with the disappearance of either the Kennedy boy or the nosy cyclist.

For the first time since Adolph had realized that he could not take all of the hogs with him in the truck, he felt that he was in control of his future.

CHAPTER 25

Carol had told Officer Damoth to take the next day off, but he was present at the squad meeting that morning, happily showing off the cast and sling on his arm and making it clear that he was raring to go back to work. Going back to work did not mean tackling the large ravine on the east lake road, however. Carol wasn't about to have a repeat of the previous day's accident. She had spent much of the previous afternoon arranging for help in the search for Martin Kennedy and Ernie Eakins from better qualified climbers in other departments and even from civilian volunteers. Inevitably, this meant finding money to cover the cost of insuring the risks involved. But she could no longer treat the two disappearances as matters outside of her jurisdiction. She had taken command of the search, and now it was her responsibility to bring it to a conclusion.

Then there was the issue of what to do with Slocomb's home on the hill. Much as she doubted that he would come back, he might do so and she wasn't sure what she was legally entitled to do on or to his property. He had never been charged with a crime and might be entirely innocent in the disappearance of Kennedy and Eakins. Her legal training and experience had never touched on anything quite like this. But she had an investigation to conduct and she couldn't sit idly by, waiting for Slocomb to reappear and take action to keep her off his property and out of his home. She had already searched his files and taken data from them regarding his business as a pork salesman. Having gone this far, why not visit the places where he had sold pork and ask questions about what kind of businessman he was?

After the squad meeting she retreated to her office and reread the list of people with whom Slocomb had done business. She knew all of them by name, and a few personally. She decided to start with the latter, beginning with Calvin Shearer at the North End Meat Market. A phone call told her that he was at the store and would be happy to see her at her convenience. What was convenient was but half an hour later, so she told JoAnne where she was going and set off to ask questions about Adolph Slocomb.

North End was a small place that, unlike most other food stores in the area, did much of its business not with major marketers but with locals in the Finger Lakes region. Calvin was the son of Roscoe Shearer who, now retired, had served the county for many years. The family had never been one of the area's most successful businesses, but it had always been respected and appreciated for its willingness to carry locally produced meat and chicken.

Calvin invited the sheriff to a small but well ordered office in the back of the store.

"So, you'd like to talk about Mr. Slocomb. Interesting chap. Is he up to something?"

It was an unexpected question, and Carol jumped at the chance to pursue Shearer's conversational initiative.

"Now that's an interesting question, Mr. Shearer. What might you have in mind? Is there something you think he could be up to?"

"Well, not really. It's just that he isn't - what shall I say? - not your usual businessman, farmer, whatever you wish to call him. I'm not criticizing him, you understand. He's honest. I've never had the feeling that he's tying to cheat me. He's one of a number of people who supply me with pork, and we get along okay."

"Glad to hear it. But I don't really know him well. In fact, I never met him until a few weeks ago on a matter that had nothing to do with the fact that he raises hogs and sells pork. So I came by to hear your assessment of him. You say he's honest. What can you tell me about him as a human being? I mean he came here not all that long ago, moved into an out of the way old house up on the hill east of the lake, and has become something of a recluse. Hard to get to know, even to talk to, if you know what I mean. How about you? Does he talk openly with you, share what's on his mind, discuss what's in the news?"

"You make it sound like there may be a problem, that he's caused - or might have caused - trouble. If not legal, maybe a personal problem with somebody here on Crooked Lake. I don't want to criticize him. Don't really know him well enough myself to do so."

"Fair enough. What brought me here is that he has left the area, or at least I think he has. I spoke with him at his house just the other day, and had a reason to go back afterwards. He wasn't there, and frankly it looks like he may have driven off with no plan to come back. That's guess work on my part, but if I were a betting person I'd say he's moved. Where to, I don't know."

"Now that's interesting," Shearer said. "He stopped here, very recently, to see if I would take some more of his pork. I was surprised. It's not the season for a sale like he had in mind, as I'm sure he knows, so I found myself wondering whether he was thinking of going out of the hog business and trying to unload some of what he had cut."

"I take it he never told you he was moving or thinking about it?"

"No, not a word."

"Okay, now a more difficult question. From your conversations with him, did you ever have the impression that Adolph might have had strong feelings about people who aren't white? You know, African-Americans, Hispanics. I'm not interested in making some kind of a judgment, only in getting a better picture of where he was coming from."

"I see." Shearer thought for a moment. "I didn't hear it from him, but somebody mentioned to me that he had hired as a handyman, or as a handyboy, a black kid whose family recently moved to Southport. If he did, it would seem to suggest that he had no negative feelings about blacks. But Adolph never talked about where he stood on issues like that."

"Or never said anything, indirectly mind you, that made you believe race or culture is important to him?"

"No, I'm afraid not. But I figured you thought that it might be, that this is why we're having this conversation."

"Maybe it was, but you're telling me that he said nothing to support my view."

"True. Funny though, that I really never knew what was on his mind. About anything except his hogs. And that he really valued his privacy."

Yes, Carol thought after leaving the North End Meat Market. His privacy. He worked hard to live in it so that he wouldn't have to reveal who he really was. And then his privacy deserted him and he realized that he had to get away so he wouldn't have to live a life that wasn't one he wanted to live.

CHAPTER 26

There were other shop keepers who purchased cuts of meat from Slocomb, and she would have to meet with them, too. But she doubted that any of them would be more helpful than Calvin Shearer. And he hadn't really been that helpful. Her conversation with him had been useful mainly because it reinforced her own impression of the hog farmer, a private person who harbored strong feelings that wanted to get out and, if released, would probably cause trouble for others. And for him. It was a problem that she needed to share with someone. Sam Bridges, of course. But more than anyone else, Kevin. Carol put up with a frustratingly slow afternoon, then hurried back to the cottage, organizing her thoughts and framing her questions as she made the drive home.

Kevin had been alerted regarding his wife's frustration, and had taken a trip to a nearby winery to replenish their stock of Chardonnay, not to mention organizing a light supper and straightening up the deck. The result was an early drink and a welcome snack as soon as Carol walked through the back door.

"It looks like you're about to put me in charge of something," he said as they took seats on the deck.

"I'm not going that far, but I do need you to hear what's happening on the law and order front. I need somebody to brainstorm with me, and your name came to mind."

"You've had a new development on the Eakins' case? Or is it the Kennedy case?"

"Let's start calling it the Slocomb case."

"He's returned from wherever he disappeared to? I thought you figured he'd vanished for good."

"I'm not sure. That's what I need to talk about."

"So now we have three disappearances."

"That's what I'm assuming, and inasmuch as he's the one most likely to tell me where Kennedy and possibly Eakins, too, have gone, I need your help in finding him."

"I thought he'd told you that the Kennedy kid had probably fallen into his ravine and that he'd never seen Eakins, didn't know who he was."

"That's true, but as time goes by I've become convinced, at least more or less convinced, that he isn't to be believed. I'm not ready to treat him as a suspect in the disappearance of our cyclist and the Kennedys' unfortunate son. But I'm afraid I'm likely to be stymied until I find him and twist his arm or whatever I have to do to make him more candid."

"But the trouble is you don't have a clue where he is. Right?"

"That's where you come in."

"I'm supposed to tell you where Slocomb is? How am I to do that? I've never even met the man. All I know is what you've told me, which is that he raises hogs and had Martin Kennedy busy doing nothing much."

"I'm not expecting that you'll bring him in, but I have to get an idea or two, and you're pretty good at coming up with ideas. Most of the time, anyway. So why not begin tonight when my own mind seems to be blank. Chardonnay usually kick starts what you call those little grey cells, so why don't you have another glass and we'll see what we can come up with."

"Okay. But you'll first have to tell me what's been going on since we last discussed the case, whatever you want to call it - Eakins' or Kennedy's or Slocomb's. Let's try this trifecta of yours."

"That's what I had in mind. As for what I've been doing, you know most of it, or at least you do if you've been paying attention. So I'll -"

"Come on, Carol. I always pay attention when you talk to me."

"Then let me briefly summarize. He's fortyish, probably not very well educated, lives in a hovel on an east shore hilltop, raises hogs and sells pork products to local grocers. He's got what I'd call a rough personality, likes his privacy, isn't very pleasant to people like me. And maybe most important, he's a white supremacist, although I don't really know whether other people around the lake know it; he doesn't talk much. But he has an unmistakable Nazi poster in his living room, a poster he doesn't seem to want his visitors to see - and he doesn't like visitors. No, that isn't quite true. He took the poster with him when he left town. Oh, and he also has a Confederate flag on his bedroom wall, so I think you can see where he's coming from. That's abut all, except for the fact that he hired an African-American boy who's got some serious mental problems to help him this summer."

"It all sounds pretty familiar. So what am I to do with the personality sketch?"

"Tell me where you think he may have gone."

"That's a big order, don't you think?"

"Well of course it is, but why not? You like to be involved in solving crimes, don't you?"

"You're putting me on, aren't you? You always tell me I'm really a professor of music."

"Yes, but I've been known to appreciate your ideas, once in awhile anyway. So come on, let's hear where you think Slocomb may have gone."

"Let's see. How about some place where he's likely to find white supremacists to hang out with, or at least make him feel at home. Given the fact that he settled here and picked a place with no class off in the boonies, I'd bet on a location where he could get away from intellectuals like us. Maybe a farm; if not hogs, how about chickens or soybeans?"

"Excuse me for being critical, but I'd suggest that you cut out the 'intellectuals like us' crap. We're normal middle class working people. If you don't believe me, take a look at our bank accounts. But otherwise what you say makes sense. Or at least it does if Slocomb didn't pick a place to live here because it was what he was used to. What if he came here to Crooked Lake to get away from some other place he'd lived, like a big city or another part of the country, and now wants to go back to something he's more familiar with, where he's more comfortable. What if farming, if you'd call raising hogs farming, was an experiment and he was tired of it?"

"The real question, I suspect, is who or what Slocomb really is. From what you tell me, he's a white racist, and from what little I know about people like that he probably has to cope with anger, maybe even rage, that white people like him are losing out and feel they have to get even. Yet he spoke with an African-American family that had recently moved to Southport and agreed to hire their retarded kid because he needed some help. Or maybe, although I doubt it, he felt sorry for the boy and thought he might be able to help him. Now that's what I would call a truly strange thing for a white racist to do. So who is this Slocomb?"

"That's the right question, but how do we find out? It seems to me that if we don't know, we'll never know where to look for him. Which means we won't find him, and if we don't we'll never know what happened to young Kennedy. And maybe to our cyclist, Ernie Eakins."

"My guess is that there's data some place, somewhere on the Internet, that would tell us where white racists and neo-Nazis are numerous and inclined to be active. If there are a lot of them and they're active all over the country, all we can do is assume that Slocomb chose to stay in the northeast and then start inquiring of police in this area if they know anything about him. Of course he could have gone to Seattle or Sacramento. Chances are we'd come up empty, either way. But what else can we do? All that I can think of is that you keep on talking with the Kennedys, hoping they will remember something that gives them a feeling, however vague, as to why Slocomb might have wanted to hire their son. Not much help, am I?"

"Don't worry. I didn't expect a big break-through suggestion. I had planned to keep talking to the Kennedys, but I'm not optimistic. What's more, it's awkward to keep reminding them of their failure to be more skeptical of Slocomb. I'll also keep on talking to the people who bought Slocomb's pork, although once again I doubt that I'll learn anything. You're right that we ought to do what we can to find out where the most active white supremacist and neo-Nazi groups are located, but wherever they are, we can hardly conduct a nation-wide search to track down Slocomb. Even the northeast, where you'd start, is a pretty big piece of real estate. With very busy police departments."

"And no reason to believe that Slocomb would visit them and divulge his plans."

"Oh, damn, I was hoping that's what he'd do. Or better yet, give me a phone call and answer my questions."

The score when they broke off this discussion and went to the dinner table was Slocomb 10, Carol and Kevin 0, although Kevin, always the more optimistic, argued for 10 to 1.

CHAPTER 27

JoAnne stuck her head into Carol's office early the next morning and passed on some news which she thought would surprise the sheriff. It did.

"Not ten minutes ago you had an interesting call. Want to guess who?"

"Now how would I know that? The president? The governor? Some Hollywood star?"

"It was another sheriff. He's calling from Blacksburg, Virginia." JoAnne watched Carol's face for a sign that she hadn't expected a call from Virginia's mountains.

Needless to say, Carol hadn't expected such a call.

"Did he say what he wanted? Am I expected to call back?"

"No to why he called, yes to a call back. Here's the number."

"Virginia. Can't imagine why."

She made the call promptly, more out of curiosity than because she thought it was important. It took longer to speak with the sheriff himself. Or herself. JoAnne had not been specific.

"This is Sheriff Prescott." It was a deep voice, with a drawl. "You're the sheriff I called a short time ago?"

"I am. I don't think I've ever talked with another sheriff in your part of the world. To what do I owe your call?"

"It's a bit complicated, so I hope you have a few minutes. First, do you recall reading about a rather nasty conflict down our way when some white supremacist protestors ran into a mob of counter protestors? It happened a couple of years ago, got a lot of press."

"Yes, I remember. Haven't heard much about it recently, but it made quite a stir when it happened. Reminded us of how divided a country we have."

"Well, that's what I'm calling about. You may have seen a follow up story about one of the people involved getting into a fight and having a coma as a result. Sound familiar?"

"Sorry. I may have read about it, but I can't be sure. Did whoever have the coma come around?"

"No he didn't, and that's what I want to talk about. Some by-stander took a photograph of the episode, so we know that the coma resulted from one of the demonstrators banging this guy's head into the pavement. Obviously this called for an arrest, but we didn't see the picture until several days after the fracas so the culprit had already slipped away. Not sure about this, but we think the man who is responsible may be in the Finger Lakes area. That's where you are, right?"

"I am. On Crooked Lake, the western Finger Lakes, not far north of the Pennsylvania border, south of Rochester. But what makes you think the man you're after is up here?"

"I'll get to that in a minute. But first, we know who he is. The photo makes it clear. His name is Michael Decker, and our research has given us a pretty good picture of him. So we've been tracking him down for months, so far without much luck. But we got a break just the other day, hence my phone call."

"Michael Decker? We're not heavily populated, but our population is large enough that I don't begin to know everybody. And off hand I don't know a Michael Decker. Glad to do what I can to find him if someone with that name lives in the area. What is it that makes you think he's on our lake?"

"I've no idea whether he's on Crooked Lake," Prescott said. "Here's the problem, or rather what we now know and what seems to put Decker in your back yard. One of his fellow white racist friends, who was with him on the day of the big demonstration, seems to have had an emotional crisis. Not that he's abandoned his commitment to the idea that white people are getting the short end of the stick in our country. But he's been bothered that Decker killed one of the liberal counter protestors during the demonstration. I think he's pretty religious, and his faith draws the line at killing people, even enemies. So one day, apparently having given the matter a lot of thought, he decided to tell us that he knew where Decker was. Or thought he was. It seems they'd been in touch. Anyway, he contacted our office and gave us Decker's area code. Naturally we tried to get more information out of him, but I guess he figured he'd satisfied his conscience by passing along the area code - you know, help the police but not really rat on his friend. The area code is 607. Does that sound familiar?"

"We're in 607, but so is quite a bit of south central New York State. So you're telling me that this guy who beat up a counter demonstrator seriously enough to kill him is, according to a semi-friend with a semi-conscience, now living in an area part of which is in my jurisdiction."

"That's just about it. I was hoping that you could look into it and see if you could help us find the man who was responsible for one of two deaths in this unfortunate melee."

"But I don't know Decker and 607 covers a lot of ground."

Carol, who had a problem of her own with a white racist, sympathized with Prescott. But - and then she had a thought. What if Slocomb was Decker, and had changed his name when he ran away from Virginia. If he had, he would have had a phone with a 607 area code.

"Does the name Adolph Slocomb mean anything to you?" she asked.

"I'm afraid not."

"A man with that name has been living here, just off Crooked Lake, for close to two years. I've gotten to know him quite well, unfortunately. And like Decker, he's very definitely a white supremacist. In fact he's a David Duke type Nazi lover. I know him because I've been investigating the disappearance of two people, and while I can't prove it, he's a suspect in one of those cases and possibly in both of them. Like Decker, he flew the coop a few days ago. What if he is Decker and changed his name to Slocomb after settling here? Without more information, that's just a wild guess, but it strikes me as one worth thinking about. Trouble is, of course, that we don't know where he is, just like you don't know where Decker is. In fact, not only don't we know where he is, we don't know what name he's using. To be of any help to you, and to me for that matter, I'll be needing more information about Decker. More than a name. Like a picture, some data about his background, his criminal record, anything that might help me know where to look for him."

Sheriff Prescott was obviously very much interested in this unexpected turn in his conversation with Sheriff Kelleher.

"I'm trying not to be too excited, but you can imagine that what you've told me is potentially good news. Maybe we ought to get together."

"I'd like that, but I'm particularly interested in meeting the man whose conscience persuaded him to give you Decker's area code. What's his name? And does he live in your area? Sometimes these white racists come from all over and get together for rallies."

Prescott thought about Carol's request and then gave her the name: Frank Walker. He was less specific about Walker's address and phone number.

"We suspect that he doesn't have a permanent home or a land line phone. I don't mean that he's homeless, only that he seems to move around, staying with a couple of women, a brother, a friend or two. Not sure why he lives like that, whether it's a money problem or that he's a permanent adolescent. Does this guy Slocomb have friends up your way I should talk to?"

"I don't think so. He's been a loner, pretty good at avoiding people. Besides, as I've told you, he packed up and left practically over night, telling no one as far as we know."

"Hmm. Sounds like we're facing similar problems."

"I'd suggest that both of us keep this conversation under our hats. Avoid linking your trouble down in Virginia with mine up here in New York. No point in helping Decker and Slocomb strategize their next move. Or *his* next move."

"Good idea. You think you'll make a trip to Blacksburg?"

"I don't know about you, but my office doesn't have a lot of cash to cover travel. However, like I said, I have two other cases to worry about, so I may have to do it. One way or another, I'll let you know what I plan to do. And I'll keep you posted if by chance I discover where Slocomb is."

"Good luck, and let's hope our country's cultural conflict settles down. I'm sympathetic to the white men who feel left out, but I can't excuse murder. Not and be a sheriff."

Carol was less sympathetic with angry white men than Prescott seemed to be. But she thought he sounded trustworthy. She also thought that she would soon be meeting him.

CHAPTER 28

Adolph Slocomb, now Kenneth Clemons, woke up to face a rainy day. It had been a bad night. The bed had been uncomfortable, and the temperature in the room had been considerably colder than the reading on the thermostat.

Why had he driven to Williamsport? He didn't want to be in Williamsport. He didn't know where he wanted to be, only that it should be far away from Crooked Lake and its nosy sheriff and bad memories. Reluctantly he crawled out of the bad bed, took a quick shower, and got into his truck for a short trip to a nearby McDonald's. The motel served breakfast, but he preferred a sausage McMuffin even if he couldn't stand the chain's annoying habit of calling everything it served as McSomething or other.

He grabbed a local paper and took a seat in a corner booth. The paper contained no news of interest, so he shoved it aside and began to think about what had become the only subject that really engaged him, the country's shabby treatment of white men who didn't work on Wall Street or otherwise lived in spacious offices in buildings called towers. The biscuit was good, but for a change the subject of white supremacy was annoying him. He was particularly annoyed that the media were calling obvious problems by unnecessary, fancy names. What bothered him most was 'alt-right.' He didn't read the *New York Times*, but he assumed that people who wrote for it used the term, and that liberals who read it enjoyed it as a highfalutin put down of people like him.

Why am I treated like white trash? Why did I have to leave Virginia because I had struck back at someone who hated what I stood for? Why did I have to leave Crooked Lake because I had gotten rid of a worthless black kid? Kenneth Clemens was angry,

angry that he was going to be using a new name, angry that he was going to have to live in a new town. His anger quickly gave way to the question of what new town he was going to have to live in. He had shoved the matter aside frequently in the last several days, but it kept coming back for the simple reason that he was on the road and couldn't stay there indefinitely.

Breakfast finished, he returned to his truck. He opened the glove compartment and took out half a dozen maps, most of which he had acquired at AAA when he began looking for a place to live when he left Virginia. He had forgotten most of the places he had considered before selecting one in the Finger Lakes. Most were in New York or Pennsylvania. A couple he had visited; most he had not. All except for Williamsport had been small, towns he had never heard of and were on his list only because they would be as unfamiliar to the Virginia police as they were to him. Where was that list? Not in the glove compartment. It would have been useful now that he had to move again. Without it, he could recall only two places other than Southport. Williamsport and North Forester. At that moment he was parked in Williamsport, or rather its suburb of South Williamsport. Why he didn't know. It was not a big city, but it was much too big for his purposes, not to mention lacking what he thought of as neighborhoods where he could live without calling attention to himself.

North Forester was another story. He couldn't remember why it had stuck in his memory. He hadn't checked it out personally, which meant that somebody he knew had recommended it. Where was it? He couldn't remember. Fifteen minutes of studying the New York and Pennsylvania maps didn't help, which meant it must be small, perhaps not even big enough to appear on a road map. He decided to drive back to the motel and use a computer he had noticed in the lobby to locate it.

It turned out to be in eastern New York, probably three or four hours drive from Crooked Lake. As he had expected, it was small - even smaller than he thought it would be, with a population of barely more than 500. Was it a community with white supremacist roots? The Google information didn't say. But he doubted that he would have remembered the name had it not had some feature that appealed to him. It took but a few minutes to make a decision to drive to North Forester. He should have done it yesterday instead of coming to Williamsport. It would take, he thought, about four hours, but he wasn't going to spend it moping around Williamsport.

It was a dreary day, the drive a dreary one. By the time he was back in New York and more than a 135 miles east of Crooked Lake, he was both tired and irritated by the fact that his windshield wipers had been at work the whole way. He saw no sign to North Forester, but he knew he was close when farm fields with barns began to give way to city houses, initially some distance apart but gradually close enough to each other to make it clear that he was entering the village. Unlike Southport, there was nothing about it to justify its place on any map. No lake, no village square, no band stand, no attractive old houses with wrap around porches that spoke of wealthy owners, but more ordinary places that presumably belonged to middle class residents. Not ideal, but he thought he could live there, especially on the outskirts.

I guess I'll drop in on the eateries, he said to himself. He had seen only two, one an old fashioned diner, the other a pizza joint. He was interested not in their food but in seeing what kind of people they were attracting. It wasn't an ideal time of day, but the cars at the curb indicated that they had a few customers.

The diner, to his surprise, was busy. Its customers looked as if they were probably a cross section of the village, mostly male (which pleased him), informally dressed. He debated taking a counter seat where he could hear what some of them were talking about, but the only available seat was between two women who were chatting with each other across the vacant seat. They were laughing, which suggested that he'd learn nothing of interest by taking that seat. He chose not to wait for a better seat, and left to visit the pizza parlor.

Only two of its tables were occupied, both by parties of four men who reminded him of regulars more interested in their beers than in their slices of pepperoni pizza. An empty table for two was close enough to both of the foursomes to lead him to select a menu and take a seat there. The noisier table attracted his attention because its occupants seemed to be engaged in an argument about whether North Forester voters should or should not accept a measure which would buy up the aged housing in some nearby block and replace it with more upscale homes. The subject might not provide information about local opinions regarding white trash, but then again it might.

One of the men, wearing Levi's and a red and blue sport shirt and sporting a large white mustache, was dominating the conversation. He appeared to feel strongly that North Forester already had too many 'monied residents,' a view which one of his colleagues thought was neither true nor very charitable. Their friends seemed content to listen. For a few minutes Clemens believed that the conversation might prove interesting. But it didn't, and he set aside his menu, told the waitress he'd changed his mind, and went back to his truck.

He quickly discovered that North Forester had no motel, and that he'd have to go another thirteen miles to find one. Instead of being annoyed with the fact that his night would have to be spent elsewhere, Clemens was pleased. The absence of a motel could mean that North Forester had few visitors, and a lack of visitors often means that money (and the attitudes that go with those who have it) are in short supply. The village was earning his respect, even if he couldn't be sure what it would be like until he had been there awhile.

Kenneth Clemens decided to postpone until the next day a more thorough investigation of his probable future home. He climbed into his truck and headed for the motel thirteen miles up the road.

CHAPTER 29

While Adolph Slocomb, now with a new name which Carol knew nothing about, was exploring a village to which he thought he might relocate, she was back on Crooked Lake, trying to learn more about him and the whereabouts of the young boy he had hired as a summer handyman.

Her immediate problems included an effort to recruit better qualified people to look for Martin Kennedy's body in Slocomb's ravine. Less important, but not to be neglected, were conversations with more of the people who had been buying the hog farmer's pork cuts. She doubted that any of them would have more to tell her than Calvin Shearer at the North End Meat Market, but she would have to pay each of them a visit.

It was while she was calling to make these appointments that she realized that it had been quite awhile since Mrs. Eakins had been in touch. Had Ernie come home? She immediately dismissed the thought. Connie would surely have called her the minute Ernie walked through the door. No, she still had two missing persons to locate, and less of a chance of finding them alive. Correct that. Three missing persons, and the third, Adolph Slocomb, was surely alive. But where was he?

Burt Hopkins, manager of a small supermarket in Yates Center, broke into her thoughts with a hearty hello.

"This is our sheriff? Well, hello. I think I met you at the store some time ago. You have a problem with something you purchased here? Sorry about that. Just bring it in and we'll make it right. Good food, good service, that's our motto."

"Thanks, Mr. Hopkins. I'll do what you suggest if ever I have a problem. But I haven't had a problem. I need to talk with you about one of your suppliers, Adolph Slocomb. Is it okay that I drop in at a convenient time?"

"Why of course." Hopkins sounded more cautious than he had when he answered the phone. "Has he done something he had no business doing with the pork he's selling?"

"Not that I know of. Can we leave the details until I can talk with you at store?"

"Of course. Come on in any time. I'm always here."

"Good. How about the lunch hour, let's say twelve, twelve-thirty."

"Looking forward to it."

Carol didn't look forward to her noon hour meeting with Burt Hopkins. She had already decided that Slocomb's customers would know very little about him because he had made it clear that he had no intention of sharing his private life with anyone. She had seen no evidence that he had any friends, and there was no reason to believe that Hopkins was an exception.

She thanked him for the offer of coffee, said no, and promised to keep their meeting brief.

"Let me begin by saying that I don't know Slocomb well at all, and that I'm here only to find out if you know him better than I do and if so in what way. So, does your relationship with him amount to anything more than buying pork from him?"

To her surprise Hopkins looked puzzled by the question. And then the puzzled look changed to an expression that Carol associated with a reluctance to answer the question.

"What is it you want to know?"

"I thought I made that clear. I want to know how well you know Slocomb other than his role as a supplier of pork."

"I'm not sure why this is important. He hasn't been in the area long, so we don't know each other well. Why should we? What's on your mind?"

It was becoming apparent that Hopkins did know Slocomb better than she had expected, or that he was simply unwilling to talk about people with whom he did business. The latter seemed more logical, but something told her that Hopkins' hesitation might have a different and perhaps more important explanation.

"Let me be more direct. And more personal. Do you know anything about Mr. Slocomb's politics?"

Carol thought Hopkins' face reddened.

"Why would I know anything about his politics? That would be none of my business."

"But maybe Slocomb brought the subject up. Maybe he wanted to know if you and he were in agreement on matters that were important to him. Would you say that you and Slocomb are pretty much like minded?"

"I really don't know. We've never talked much, and now he's moved away."

Now how would you know that, Carol asked herself.

"Slocomb's moved away? When did he do that, and where did he go?"

Hopkins suddenly looked uneasy.

"Oh, I assumed that you'd know about his moving. It happened just the other day. But of course I don't know where he went."

"How did you learn about this?"

"He wanted to sell me some pork. He couldn't move his hogs with him, so he was thinking about slaughtering them all and selling the choice cuts. But I couldn't help him. Wrong time to stock up, so I had to say no thanks."

"Did he tell you why he was moving away from Crooked Lake?"

It had finally dawned on Burt Hopkins that the sheriff's interest in Slocomb had to do with his moving, and that in all probability she already knew about it before making an appointment to see him.

"Not exactly."

"How about less than exactly?"

"Okay, he wasn't happy to be making another move so soon after settling here and starting up a fairly decent business."

"That I can understand, but it still doesn't explain why he did it. I'd appreciate it if you'd tell me exactly what he said when he told you he was leaving Crooked Lake."

"Not much, really. Mostly he seemed to be unhappy that his house - it was way up on a hill between here and Watkins - attracted too many people. At least too many people he didn't much care for. He was a loner, didn't like company, but he was getting too much of it. Thought he'd see if he could get away from people somewhere else."

"Did he mention any of these people he didn't care for?"

Hopkins was not comfortable with these questions and said so.

"Look, I'm not a close friend of his, but I don't like to talk about a personal conversation. He'd surely prefer that I not share what he talked about without his permission. Like I said, he's a private person."

"Was one of these people he didn't much care for the sheriff? Me?"

Hopkins face reddened again.

"Well, he did say you'd been to see him a number of times. I suppose just about anyone would be nervous if the sheriff kept coming around." Hopkins laughed nervously. "But he didn't criticize you."

"Did he mention any other people?"

"He talked about a black family in town. Can't remember the name, but their son worked for him."

"If a member of that family had been hired by Slocomb, why would he mention the family as people he didn't care for?"

Hopkins looked as if he wished he'd never agreed to meet with the sheriff.

"I guess it was because he didn't like black people. Mr. Slocomb was one of those whites who don't much like that this is becoming a polyglot society."

"Polyglot? People using different languages?" Carol couldn't recall ever hearing anyone use the word. But now the manager of a local supermarket had done so.

"Well, something like that. Not just old familiar Anglo-Saxons, but Chicanos, Asians, blacks of course. Like this country, it was all Europeans for centuries, but then a big and growing minority of outsiders started coming here. Slocomb was convinced that this minority was going to become a majority unless -"

"Yes, unless what?"

"He didn't say."

"He's a white racist, don't you suppose?

"I wouldn't go that far. After all, he'd hired that black kid."

"May I point out that the African-Americans who live here didn't come to the United States of their own free will. They are here because their ancestors were brought here against their will as slaves. But let's leave that aside for now. How do you explain that this man, who liked his privacy and didn't talk much, shared his views about other cultures with you? Because he saw in you someone who agreed with him?"

"Now wait a minute, sheriff. Our constitution gives all of us a right to our opinions, the right to say what we believe. That's good, don't you think? Your job is to uphold the law, and it's the law I'm talking about. So why are you pestering me now? I haven't done anything illegal."

"I'm glad to hear it. That's fine, as long as thoughts and words don't turn to violence."

What Carol had expected to be a simple conversation had turned into an unpleasant discussion that had made it clear that Slocomb had at least one friend on Crooked Lake, and that both he and his friend might qualify as white racists. She wondered if there might be more 'friends of Slocomb' around the lake. And if Slocomb's thoughts and words had ever crossed the line into violence.

CHAPTER 30

It had't been easy, but Carol was ultimately able to free up the necessary money for a trip to Blacksburg, Virginia. Making the trip necessitated a call to Sheriff Prescott to make sure that Frank Walker had not, like Adolph Slocomb, skipped town, and would be willing to meet with her. It took Prescott two days to locate Walker and persuade him to talk with another sheriff.

"He's not happy to have his conversation with me draw him deeper into this case. I had to remind him several times that he's got to cooperate with me (and you, unfortunately) if he wishes to avoid getting into real trouble. I think these guys who live on the edge of racial violence tend to think they have the Constitution to protect them from us law and order types. They've done their homework, know what they can do and whom to blame if things get out of hand. But they're so committed to their cause, and so confident that it's got the support of key big wigs, that they're always courting trouble. Like the Bundy clan and its sagebrush rebels and their conflict with the Bureau of Land Management out west. Anyway, Walker says he'll talk to you. Just be careful."

When Carol got to Blacksburg and proceeded to the address Prescott had given her, she found both Walker and the sheriff waiting for her. Probably Prescott had decided that unless he was there to make sure Walker would honor his agreement, her trip would be a waste of both time and money.

Carol had done something she doubted she had ever done before, something that might give her an advantage but nonetheless made her uncomfortable. She had left her uniform at home and worn a pair of beige slacks and a blue blouse. The mirror at the cottage told her that she looked good, even slightly sexy. She hoped it would impress Walker.

She introduced herself to both of them. The sheriff was younger than she had expected. She found herself feeling momentarily somewhat depressed that she was almost certainly older than he was. Walker was also younger; Prescott had said he was about thirty. That was what had led to her decision to leave her uniform at home. Based on stories she had read in the papers, she had been of the opinion that Millennials were likely to be a progressive, open minded generation. If so, Walker was an exception, at least politically. But he might be like many men when they found themselves in an attractive woman's presence.

There was no point in spending much time getting to know Prescott. She could talk with him later. Instead, she concentrated on the young white racist.

"Thanks for being willing to spend some time with me. You have given me an opportunity to visit this delightful part of our country. It's a first for me. But of course I'm really here because Mr. Prescott had told me that you know Michael Decker and that you participated in a demonstration here awhile back. Which means that you may be able to help me solve a problem I'm facing where I work back in New York state."

Walker gave her a smile but said nothing.

"Let me begin by letting you know about my problem." Carol explained her need to find a man named Slocomb and that she suspected he might be the man Walker knew as Michael Decker. "You know Decker. Do you also know someone named Slocomb? Or should I say do you believe that Decker has changed his name to Slocomb? This is very important, not just to me but more importantly to the parents of their son, a young boy who was working for Mr. Slocomb. You see, that boy has disappeared, which makes it of critical importance that I talk to this man Slocomb."

"Maybe the boy you talk about is missing because he went somewhere with Mr. Slocomb."

"I'm afraid not. He's been missing for a couple of weeks. Mr. Slo-comb disappeared just two or three days ago." Carol moved forward to the edge of her chair and crossed her legs. Walker's eyes followed her as she moved. "You see, it's possible, if not certain, that the young man is dead and that Mr. Slocomb is responsible for his death. This is the kind of case that worries sheriffs. We want to bring wrong doers to justice, but it's equally necessary that we protect the innocent. And at the moment Mr. Slocomb is innocent. I'm hoping you can help me determine whether he is or isn't."

"And how am I supposed to help you?"

"The more you can tell me about Michael Decker - about whether the man I'm looking for might be him - the more I'll know about the case I'm trying solve up in New York. You told Sheriff Prescott that you had come to him because your religion is very much against killing. Mine is, too. We may have enemies, but we talk to them, reason with them; we don't kill them. It sounds to me that the way you handled what Mr. Decker did during a demonstration down here was the right thing to do. It wasn't only right, it was brave because none of us likes to be guilty of criticizing our friends."

Walker shrugged his shoulders, and his smile reappeared.

"How, by the way, did you know that Mr. Decker had moved to New York state, that you could reach him on Crooked Lake?"

"I didn't know where he was until *he* called me. He had sort of taken me under his wing while he lived here. Treated me like a son he never had. At least that's what he told me, and he seemed honest. Anyway, when he called, I thought it was appropriate to share my religious convictions. He took it very well, said I was right, that our relationship was a two way street. I remember that he confessed to not ever having gone to church. Anyway, he said he'd become a believer, that Jesus would now be his guide."

Carol couldn't accept this without a question.

"Did he say he'd abandoned his white racist philosophy?"

Walker looked as if he wasn't sure what a philosophy was. But then his face broke into another smile. "Oh, I see what you mean. No, quite the contrary. He said that it was white people who were the true Christians."

There was no need to tell him that this was ridiculous.

"Why did he call you?"

"At first I thought it was just to say hello, tell me he was okay. But he went on to tell me, sort of indirectly, where he was and that he'd run into some other guys who were on our side of what he calls the 'culture war.' His only complaint was that they weren't as well organized as we were down in Virginia. Just before he rang off he brought up another reason for calling, that he was going to move again. He didn't say to where, only that he'd stay in touch. It was kinda funny, his telling me he was moving. He'd never told me about the first move, the one from which he made the call."

"Did he tell you he'd changed his name? Did he say he was now Adolph Slocomb?"

"That's what you think, isn't it?" Walker said.

"What I'm asking is whether he said so."

"No, he didn't. I never heard about this man named Slocomb until you mentioned him."

Carol could think of no reason why Walker would be lying about this, but then she didn't know much about what was going on in Slocomb's head. If the man they were talking about was Slocomb. In any event, she realized that she hadn't learned much from Walker - not that Slocomb was Decker, not where Slocomb had moved to from Crooked Lake. All she was sure of was that Walker had spent a lot of time trying - unsuccessfully - to avoid staring at her (and maybe wondering why a sheriff was a woman, not wearing a uniform and not carrying a gun). What would Kevin say when she told him she had not worn her uniform, and why she hadn't?

After Walker had gone, she spent another fifteen minutes with Sheriff Prescott.

"Thanks, Mr. Prescott," Carol said when with Walker's departure they had the room to themselves. "It was a useful discussion, even if he didn't provide all of the information I had hoped for. Considering his politics and his religious beliefs, he's in something of a bind. But unless he's not being straightforward, he also doesn't know that much about Decker. Which means that you and I don't know if Decker is now calling himself Slocomb. Or maybe something else. And where he is, and that's a big issue for both of us. This is a big country; he could be anywhere."

"What's your hunch, sheriff?" Prescott asked. "About Decker being Slocomb, I mean."

"I don't like to guess. It's too easy to talk yourself into believing something that may not be true, and the first thing you know you're heading down the wrong road."

"Yeah, I know the problem. I'll try to avoid assuming my man is really your Slocomb, but my gut feeling tells me there's a good chance he is. In which case we're now working on the same case."

"If so, I hope it'll be a successful adventure," Carol said. "In any event, thanks for bringing me up to date on the crisis you've been facing since Decker and his buddies had their demonstration down here."

"You probably don't have our problem up in New York. This is a pretty conservative area, a lot of people still fighting the Civil War. Being sheriff in this neighborhood makes you watch your step."

Carol didn't know what conclusions to draw from this remark. But she felt obligated to wish Prescott well and assume that she and he were on the same side of this issue.

CHAPTER 31

Kenneth Clemens (a.k.a. Michael Decker and Adolph Slocomb) awoke from a bad night in a bad motel with the sky still dark and a pounding headache. The headache probably had something to do with too many beers, but Clemens knew that the real reason was disappointment with North Forester as the choice for his new home. He could still change his mind and continue his search for a safe place to live. But the thought only made his headache worse. North Forester might buy him time; it might even keep the police from his door indefinitely. But it would almost certainly deprive him of a chance to participate in the campaign for white supremacy, for putting a stop to the mongrelization of the United States. Perhaps he should stop looking for a place to hide and become instead a more openly vocal advocate for a cause he felt strongly about.

But as he looked at his face in the mirror while shaving, Clemens realized that he didn't have the courage to put himself in a position that could lead to a long incarceration in some prison, probably in New York but possibly in Virginia. He'd either have to settle for North Forester, at least for the near term, or set off on the road again in search for a better hiding spot.

"Damn it!" he cursed. "What a rotten country we've become."

The unpleasantness of his situation only became worse as he drove back to North Forester. There were no places to eat, not at this hour. He doubted that he'd find one at any hour, which meant that he'd do his own cooking, something he'd done on Crooked Lake but never enjoyed. The morning sky was brightening, but the area he'd chosen for his new home lacked activity. And he had already decided that he wouldn't go back to hog slaughtering as a way to make a living. Which brought to mind another, perhaps even more serious problem. What was he going to do to pay for where he was living, assuming that he did find a place to live? Crooked Lake didn't have much, but a couple of hours in North Forester had already told him that it had even less.

The town wasn't deserted, but there were few people out and about on its streets. What did residents of North Forester do? It was a question he often asked himself as he drove through scantily populated areas. It was too early to begin stopping at places which looked as if they might be for sale or be a rental possibility. All he could do was drive around the town, up one street and down another, plus the suburbs. He laughed at the idea of suburbs. To be in a suburb, houses had to be some distance from a town center, and no house he had passed coming into North Forester and departing for the motel was more than a quarter of a mile from the excuse for a town center. His eye open for 'For Sale' or 'For Rent' signs, Clemens covered every street in North Forester in less than about twenty minutes. He saw nothing to indicate that this sleepy town had anything which qualified as a vacancy. He had, however, passed a house with a sign on its lawn saying that it was the home of a Real Estate Agent.

That the agent, if he were at home, would be of any help was doubtful, but at this stage of the search there was no reason not to make an inquiry. It was only 9:15, but Clemens had no interest in delaying the inquiry until mid-morning or afternoon. If the agent were missing (or still in bed), he'd try to get something for breakfast at the diner.

It was more than five minutes after he first rang the bell that someone came to the door. The someone was dressed, but in Levi's and a button-up sweater he didn't look ready to discuss the housing market.

"Good morning, sir. What's the problem?" His voice made it clear that he was surprised to have company.

"I'm sorry if I've gotten you out of bed, but I'm new to your town and I need a place to stay. Your sign suggests that maybe you can help me."

The surprised look was replaced by a sad smile.

"We really need a motel, but since the *Best Western* failed three years ago we've had to manage without one. There is one in Babcock, however. Just a few miles up the road."

"I'm not interested in a motel. I'm looking for a house, probably a rental, not a bed for the night. Do you suppose that there's any place here in North Forester that might be available?"

"You thinking of moving here, maybe have some business that brings you this way?"

Clemens was annoyed with the agent, but prepared to accept his questions as an admission that North Forester was on its last legs.

"Look, my reason for being at your door isn't important. Why don't you just regard me as someone who's here to see if you can help him find a place to live. I don't see much evidence that places are for sale or for rent, but I'm here to see if I might be wrong."

"Well, the market has been mighty slow. Things could change, but I gather that you're not in a position to wait for one of our residents to move to Albany or someplace else. The only thing I can suggest is Sarah Kimbrough. She owns a place on Crown Street, east side of town. I know she's not about to sell. That'd be the day. But people talk, and they say she thinks from time to time about taking in a roomer. It's a fairly big house, and she had a bit of remodeling done after her husband died. Truth is, I've never talked to her about it. Too ornery, probably would tell me to leave her alone. But she might be willing to talk with you, and it's you not me that needs a place to live."

The idea of taking a room in an old house in North Forester had never occurred to Clemens. It wasn't something that lifted his spirits. If you like your privacy, the last thing you want to do is move in with a stranger, especially a stranger who makes the rules of coming and going and maybe more. But he was in a pickle, and he didn't know anything about this Kimbrough lady. He obviously didn't have a lot of options, and it might turn out to be a temporary arrangement.

"Tell me where she lives."

"Crown Street is the second road behind me, here in the heart of town. Mrs. Kimbrough has a place on the corner of Shaker Boulevard."

"Streets here are called boulevards?"

"Just a way to liven things up."

"I think I'll pay the old lady a visit," Clemens said. "Thanks for the advice. I doubt I'll take a room there, and from what you say I doubt she'll want a roomer. Have a good day."

"Oh, I forgot to tell you one thing. Better do it, just so you won't be surprised." The real estate agent's sign had said his name was Sargent, and Sargent was now wearing a smile. "Mrs. Kimbrough's not an old lady. Just a guess, but I'd say she's in her late thirties. No more than forty."

"Thanks for the head's up."

His watch said that it was now about 9:50. The news that Mrs. Kinbrough was of an age not far from his own had not been a breath of fresh air. Quite the contrary. It made the former Adolph Slocomb nervous. Before parking his truck and ringing her doorbell, Clemens drove up the boulevard and slowly down Crown Street past the Kimbrough house. It was not a particularly distinguished house. The paint job was not ancient, but probably dated back nine or ten years. The grass needed mowing, but Kimbrough, according to the presence of attractive flower beds, obviously enjoyed gardening, The porch contained three large wicker chairs and the morning paper, which, while uncollected, suggested that the owner was at home.

He circled the 'heart of town' one more time and then parked at the curb three houses from the Kimbrough place. He picked up the paper and rang the bell.

The woman who came to the door was wearing a pink and white robe and pink slippers. She was of average height for a woman, and her hair, while still unbrushed, was attractive. She was doing just what he was doing: sizing up the person on the other side of the entrance.

"Yes?"

At first he wasn't sure just what to say, this in spite of the fact that he often had reacted in much the way she had when someone came to the door.

"I'm sorry to bother you," he finally said, "but I'm new to town and I have a problem."

"And what is your problem?"

Clemens took a deep breath.

"I need a place to stay, and I've heard that you might be willing to take in - maybe I should say to put up a roomer. Am I wrong?"

"I've never welcomed roomers. I have space, but I enjoy my privacy. So why is it that you are asking me to let you stay here?"

"There doesn't seem to be any other place to stay in North Forester."

"How long is it that you need to stay in North Forester?"

"I don't really know. It depends."

"On what?"

"At the moment I'm not quite sure." Clemens was beginning to sweat.

"I might be willing to make an exception," she said, a smile appearing on her face. "But let me tell you something, Mr. - Mr. what? You haven't told me your name. In fact, you haven't answered any of my questions. Why am I expected to give up my privacy so you can have a place to stay, for how long neither of us seems to know? If you think I'll be inviting you to have some kind of relationship with me, forget it. Do you understand me?"

"Of course. All I need is a place to sleep.."

"And eat? Fine, if you use the microwave in the bedroom. I don't cook for strangers."

To his surprise, the ice had apparently been broken.

"That's very kind of you. What are your terms, Mrs. Kimbrough?"

"Yes, my name is Kimbrough. I assume that you got it from Sargent, our local real estate agent. And you are?"

"Kenneth Clemens."

"Okay, Mr. Clemens. My terms are thirty dollars a day plus work I need done around the house. Like fixing the kitchen drain and some rewiring that's long overdue."

He didn't like to be treated like that, but in the circumstances he knew he had no choice.

"I accept. Now if I can have a key, I'll move my stuff in."

"I'll give you a key, but first I want two hundred ten dollars; that's the first week's advance."

Clemens, struggling to keep his anger under control, pulled a thick wad of bills from his pocket and counted out $210.

"Here!" he said as he handed them over. This was going to be a much more difficult arrangement than the one he had had on his hog farm above Crooked Lake.

CHAPTER 32

He had retrieved his truck and reparked it at the curb in front of the Kimbrough house. It was obvious that there wasn't going to be any off-street parking for him in North Forester, not unless he wanted to argue the matter with Mrs. Kimbrough, and that was an argument he was sure he wouldn't win. The house had two front doors, the main one where he and she had talked, a less impressive one that looked as if it had been added years after the house had been built, probably after the husband's death. In any event, that was the one in which his key worked. Clement opened the door and found himself in a modest room which was sparsely furnished but was considerably more attractive than the one he had occupied on the hilltop outside of Southport. The furniture consisted of a queen-sized bed, a bedside table with lamp on it, a dresser which would be more than adequate for his limited wardrobe, a large chair that looked comfortable, behind which was a tall floor lamp. The walls contained no pictures, which interestingly had the effect of making the room look larger than it really was. To his right, toward Shaker Boulevard, was a small bathroom and a table that might hold a computer and did hold a coffee maker and a microwave. Beside it on the floor was a small refrigerator, resting on cinderblocks. Sarah Kimbrough may not have wanted boarders, but she had redone this corner of the house to accommodate them if she changed her mind.

Why she had changed her mind he did nor know. Perhaps she had lied about not being interested in 'relationships' with boarders. Perhaps she had seen him as a candidate for an affair. If so, he did not share her interest. It was obvious that the remodeling that had taken place after her husband's death had included removing the door to the adjacent room, meaning that for her to enter his room or him to enter the rest of the house they would have to do so from the porch. Kenneth - for that was what he had to call him-self now - went around the room, testing the bed (fairly hard), the lights (both operating), the other appliances (obviously new and ready for use). What maintenance jobs for him did she have? He suspected that they might only be her way of reminding him that he would be living in her house and responding to her beck and call.

He brought his few belongings in from the truck and stored them either in the dresser or on one of the small tables. For a brief minute he debated whether to put the Nazi poster on one of the walls. It would be a welcome addition to the bland room, but he had no idea whether Kimbrough would tolerate it. In fact he had no idea whether the owner would let herself into his room. He was sure that he would not be invited into any of her rooms, not that he cared. What he cared most about was how much time he would be spending in this out of the way town with a woman he found annoying.

While he was considering the situation in which he found him-self, he heard a knock on the door.

'Damn woman,' he said under his breath. 'I'll bet she'll never leave me alone.' He opened the door and watched as Kimbrough crossed the carpeted floor to the big chair and took a seat. She had dressed, and he was aware that while she was beginning to show her age, she was still a good looking woman with a good figure.

"I thought it would be a good idea to get started on that repair work I mentioned. It's not necessary that it be started today. You probably need to take a day or two to familiarize yourself with our town, take a shower, you know, become a North Forester. But the work I have in mind is overdue, and I thought I would tell you about it so you could visit the hardware store and pick up any tools and materials you'll be needing. So why don't we take a look at the situation over in my place. I have to go out pretty soon - so let's do it now."

He had hoped that the repairs she had spoken of could wait for weeks, possibly forgotten altogether. No such luck. That he would have to supply whatever would be needed to do the work made him even more irritated by his new land lady. He'd like to tell her to get out, to let him have a nap or some lunch. But he bit his tongue.

"Of course. I hope that the job is a small one."

"Well, it's really several jobs. I'm not an expert on these things, so I have no idea about how long they'll take. Why don't you use the john if you must, then we'll be off."

Clemens clenched his teeth. 'My God,' he thought, 'the bitch is going to sit there in my chair while I take a piss.' He closed the bathroom door behind him, trying unsuccessfully not to slam it too hard. It was going on eleven o'clock when he slid into the passenger seat of Kimbrough's Corolla and they set of for downtown North Forester.

Sarah, for that's what she insisted he call her, had shown him what he had to do, and since he had worked all his life with his hands and had a good idea of what these jobs would require and how long they would take, he made the necessary purchases. Sarah obviously had no intention of footing the bill. It came to $162.19.

Neither of them had anything to say on the way back to Crown Street, although she did manage to thank him for 'taking care of my problems.' Clemens was hungry. Instead of reentering his small pad he decided to walk back to the diner; it seemed better than to take a mere three minute drive to fill his stomach. It also gave him time to speculate on whether Sarah would take advantage of the fact that he had gone out for lunch to see what he had brought with him to North Forester. If she had done so, she would certainly be disappointed.

The lunch hour also gave him an opportunity to think about the problem of what he was going to do to pay Sarah's thirty dollars a day fee. The wad of bills in his pocket would last awhile, perhaps for a month or two. If she paid him for the repair work, it might cover his costs for another few weeks, but nothing she had said suggested that she had any intention of paying for his labor. Maybe other residents of the town might do so. He hadn't considered that possibility previously, but now that he possessed a few basic tools - his, not her's - it might be a good idea to check whether there was some way to advertise his willingness to be a handyman for North Forester locals.

The thought reminded him of Martin Kennedy, a handyman he had hired for a pittance a few weeks earlier. A handyman he didn't need, a black handyman whom he had hoped might in time become a sort of 21st century slave. Clemens chuckled. It had been a stupid idea, and he had made it impossible by killing the boy rather than risk letting him tell his parents about the 'trouble' at the hog farm. He briefly let his mind wander to Crooked Lake and the sheriff he hated. What was she doing now that he had disappeared, much as Kennedy and the cyclist had? Still looking for them? In all probability that was what she was doing. She was tenacious if not terribly smart. Odds were that she would find the boy, but it would do her no good. He had died because he was mentally retarded and didn't know enough not to walk off the ledge into the ravine. And she'd never find the cyclist or any evidence that he'd ever been on Adolph Slocomb's property.

The white supremacist who had killed three people in less than three years was not looking forward to going back to the house on Crown Street and becoming a member of yet another dismal community. But he was safe there, with a name that would mean nothing to the cops in Virginia or New York's Finger Lakes, and in time what had happened in those places would have become old stories, closed cases in the nation's culture wars which people like him were gradually winning.

CHAPTER 33

While Adolph Slocomb, now Kenneth Clemens, was contemplating a temporary career as a repair man, Sheriff Kelleher was getting ready for a new search of the large ravine to the south of Slocomb's old abode and hog pen. But this time it was not her officers that would be tackling the job. She had contacted several Cumberland County companies that reportedly had services that included work of the kind she wanted done. She knew the owners of two of these companies and finally had hired one of them to continue the search for Martin Kennedy.

"It'll be a piece of cake," Dick Stacy assured her. " How about this coming Saturday?"

The day was agreeable to her, but she thought Stacy was too optimistic about the task he would be undertaking. In any event, Stacy had his men, along with a couple of trucks with cranes, at the ravine site early on Saturday morning. Fortunately, the rain which had been forecast was not yet falling. She and Bridges were present to observe and, if necessary, to offer advice.

Their advice was not needed. Seventy-five minutes after beginning the search, one of Stacy's men shouted from his perch on a crane that he could see a male body lodged in a tree about three dozen feet above his head. It had been trapped in a fork of the tree and looked to him as if it might stay wedged there for a considerable length of time. It took the crew about forty minutes and some difficult rope work to rescue the late Martin Kennedy from the place where his fall down the ravine had ended.

From the moment she first heard the workman's shout, Carol knew that the boy was dead, that she would be the bearer of bad news to Ruth and Henry Kennedy. But she was quite sure that they had already come to the conclusion that their son was dead and had done their best to steel themselves for her confirmation of what they had feared.

The rest of the morning was devoted to bringing Martin's body to earth and then to transfer it first to the ambulance Carol had called and then to the morgue in Yates Center. It was not possible to tell from her observation as a layman just what had been the cause of death - whether the fall had killed Martin or whether he had been killed before his killer had shoved him into the ravine. Another autopsy would have to be performed, and once again she would have to find someone to perform it. Doc, where are you when I need you? This didn't look like 'the woman in the wall' case where she had to bring in a specialist from Rochester. Perhaps Doc Crawford could be persuaded to come out of retirement for what should be a simple autopsy. Thank goodness, his cancer was under control, or so he had insisted, and she'd be able to call on his long time ties to her family to help bring this frustrating case closer to conclusion. She'd give him a call.

But first she'd have to see the Kennedys, and do so before any autopsy had been performed. She reluctantly hoped that Martin's death was due to the fact that he had lost his footing and plunged into the ravine. She could not imagine that his parents would prefer to hear that someone, almost certainly Slocomb, had killed him and gotten rid of his body. Much as she herself had come to loath Slocomb, she preferred that an autopsy would not increase the likelihood that he had become a two time killer.

When she got back to the office, her first call was to Officer Damoth, now back to his regular duty on county highways.

"Thought I'd let you know that we found the Kennedy boy," she told him. "I'm so sorry that I didn't try some tree trimmers before you broke your arm in that damn ravine."

"I was afraid that's what would happen," he replied. "Try to be a hero and all you get is a trip to the hospital. But I know you've been worried about the kid. And I assume he was dead."

"I'm afraid so. I always thought it would turn out like this. But there's still a chance that you'll be in on a man hunt for a killer. Depends on an autopsy I've got to arrange."

"I thought your money was on an accidental fall into that ravine."

"My hope was for an accident. But it's too soon to say case closed. I'll let you go. Don't break another arm."

Carol's next call was to the Kennedys, and it was a call that she dreaded. Ruth answered.

"Mrs. Kennedy, I'm calling to share some bad news with you. We have discovered your son, or I'm afraid I should say we've discovered his body. I'm so terribly sorry. Would it be possible for me to come by your house and talk with you and your husband?"

"I've been afraid of this, sheriff. In fact, Henry and I have been pretty sure that we'd never see Martin again. I'm not quite sure when it was that we gave up hope, but it got to the point that we could no longer see how he could have just disappeared. I still cry sometimes. I'll probably do so for a long time to come. But yes, we'd be grateful if you came by, although I'm not sure we need to hear the details. Maybe Henry will. He's not here right now. Would you be able to come by, say, around five this afternoon?"

"I'll be there. I'm so sorry, but I had to let you know. If you or your husband decide you aren't up to it, please leave me a message. I'll understand."

Having told JoAnne when she'd be leaving, Carol tried Dr. Crawford, who turned out to be at home and bored with inactivity.

"You've been ignoring me, Carol."

"Hardly. I've been trying to let you enjoy your retirement."

"Retired or not, I always appreciate a call from you. What's new?"

"I'm not sure how to say this, Doc, but would you be willing to play pathologist one more time and do a simple autopsy for me?"

"I could have guessed this. Well, you're timing couldn't be better. I really am retired, but my cancer is in remission and you say this is a simple case, so I suppose I ought to say yes. Besides, I've already told you I'm bored, so how can I refuse? But tell me, what do you mean by simple? I thought you did the simple ones yourself."

"Doc, I never do autopsies, simple or complex. But I think this one shouldn't be much of a problem. A young man, about fifteen, was found in a ravine over on the east lake road. He probably fell and the fall caused his death. Unfortunately, it's possible, if not likely, that somebody killed him and threw his body down the ravine. So I'd be asking you to study the body and let me know whether there's a chance that I'll be investigating a murder."

"You have as much of a chance of avoiding murders as I do avoiding boredom in retirement, don't you?"

"The odds are that this won't be a murder, Doc. All I'm doing - all I'm asking you to do - is confirm my hunch that I'm confronting an accidental death. That's likely, inasmuch as the boy is or was handicapped. He had down's syndrome, not to mention something called autism spectrum disorder. So you see he was a very troubled kid, somebody who could very easily have fallen into a very deep ravine."

"Then why are you talking to me about an autopsy?"

"Because he was working for a nasty man who happens to be a white supremacist. And the boy was an African American. You get the picture? Why would somebody who loves Nazis and the KKK hire a young black handyman who's mentally retarded? And who skips town as soon as I begin to put pressure on him?"

"I see. This isn't a normal case, is it? But then you're always confronting me with abnormal cases. You're sure you want me to find that this is an accidental death?"

"I want you to find out what happened to young Martin Kennedy. That's the boy's name. My job is to find the guy who hired him and - you're going to love this - killed somebody else a year or two ago down in Virginia in a white rage demonstration."

CHAPTER 34

When Carol got off the phone with Doc Crawford, she had a thought that initially puzzled her and then worried her. It had to do with the fact that Adolph Slocomb had told her that he had not been at his home throughout the day when Martin Kennedy had disappeared. He had been visiting stores in the Crooked Lake area that carried his pork. It had been a reasonable explanation for his inability to tell her what had happened to Martin. For the first time, she was regretting her acceptance of Slocomb's story. She should have been skeptical sooner, and now it might be too late.

Having spent much of the day on the phone already, she managed to do quite a bit more calling in the afternoon before going to the Kennedys, hoping to comfort them in their loss. The people she spoke with this time were the shop keepers who purchased Slocomb's pork. And the first of these had been Burt Hopkins, who didn't say so in so many words when she had first spoken to him but had left the impression that, like Slocomb, he could be a white supremacist.

Hopkins was obviously surprised to hear from the sheriff again. He seemed even more surprised to be asked if Slocomb had visited his store on the date that the hog farmer had said he had done so. The question produced no certain answer.

"I'm not sure. My suppliers come at various times and I don't always write down the dates. Adolph may have come by then, but I really don't remember."

Asked if he might have a log book in which he kept such information, Hopkins gave the matter some thought before again retreating into uncertainty. It quickly became apparent that Hopkins was not going to help Carol with information about what Slocomb was doing the day that Martin Kennedy went missing.

Whether he could if he wanted to or was protecting his friend was another matter. Frustrated but not entirely surprised, Carol turned her attention to the other names on the list of Slocomb's customers.

The results were inconclusive. Two were unavailable, one, like Hopkins, couldn't be sure. But Jack Sickles was sure he hadn't seen Slocomb on that day but several days later. What is more he had a written record which 'proved it.' Unlike all but one of the other of Slocomb's customers he expressed mild curiosity as to why the sheriff was asking him the question.

"Just that he mentioned to me that he visited the stores that bought his products back then."

"Well, he must have gotten his dates mixed up."

"Did this happen often? I mean, did you and he have a routine?"

"I thought so, but of course any of us can have problems that upset a schedule."

And so the sheriff was left with the impression that Slocomb might well have done what he said he had done, but that maybe he hadn't. Frustrated, she set the list of his customers back on the desk. This time it was upside down, and there, staring at her, was a name that was barely legible. She leaned over her desk and squinted at the word, actually two words, that had been scrawled there. It read North Forester. It was vaguely familiar, but meant nothing to her. But it was on the opposite side of the list of Slocomb's customers she had just called, so she continued to stare at it. Yes, it did say North Forester. And it didn't register as the name of any place she had ever heard of. Was it even a place? The word North suggested as much. Forester didn't. People were foresters; towns we're not. But could they be?

Carol, being Carol, was interested. She walked down to Officer Byrnes' office.

"Hi, Tommy. I've got a question for you, and if you can't answer it, a mission."

"I hope it's not a mission impossible."

"I doubt it, knowing something about your skills as a searcher. It has to do with words I saw on the back of a list of food stores in our area. Food stores where Mr. Slocomb - remember him? - sold pork to their meat departments."

Carol took a seat and pulled the paper with the badly scrawled North Forester from her pocket.

"What does that look like to you?"

Tommy looked at it carefully.

"North Forester. I've no idea what it means."

"North suggests that it's a place. Ever hear of someplace with a name like that?"

"No, but then this is a pretty big country. If it is a place, that is. May not even be the United States. The Brits might have a place name like that. Or the Irish. Or maybe it isn't a place name. Can you think of anything else?"

"Not off hand, which is why I'm letting you take a crack at it."

"I'll give it a try. And start with places, like villages. I'll go with the US, not overseas somewhere."

"Okay. And if I were you I'd start with places in the east. Inasmuch as Slocomb probably wrote it and he's been living in the east. Just a guess, you understand."

Reasonably sure that Byrnes was more likely than any of her other men to find out what North Forester was and where it was, Carol wished him luck and went back to her own office. It was only ten minutes later that he buzzed her.

"Not sure that this is the answer to your puzzle," he said. "But I started with New York State, that being where we are. And there is a North Forester in our state. Nowhere near here, but I thought I'd tell you about it before I went off on some other tangent."

Carol was both impressed by the report and pleased that Tommy had found a possible answer to her question so quickly.

"It's not much of a place, but a few minutes ago we didn't even know if North Forester was a place name. Now here's what I've learned. Our state has a small village with that name. It's down state, meaning it's east of the Hudson River, not too far from Red Hook. Not much about it on the computer, probably because it's so small and, I assume, because nothing about it appears to be important. By small I mean a few hundred people; by unimportant I mean it had no distinguished residents or former residents or landmarks. If you think you'd like to look at a map, I've got one that should do. I'm going to take a look at the other 49 states to see if one of them has a North Forester."

"Any info that mentions why this little village has that odd name?"

"Unfortunately no. And there's no South Forester, or East or West Forester on any map."

"North Forester may mean nothing, but in the circumstances I can't dismiss it as a meaningless jotting. Let me know if you find anything else which may be relevant. Then we'll start picking the village apart, looking for anything that might tell us if Slocomb has any reason to be interested in it."

"It doesn't sound very promising, but then I know nothing about this Slocomb character. Or North Forester. I'll let you know if I discover anything else. I wouldn't bet on it."

The sheriff resumed her study of the phrase North Forester, turning the scrawled name around to better read it from every angle. It still meant nothing to her. Did it mean something to Adolph Slocomb? Carol knew that she couldn't wait until Byrnes had learned whether a North Forester existed in any of the other states of the union. She'd have to learn more about North Forester, New York. And right away. But first she had a responsibility to the Kennedys.

CHAPTER 35

"Hello, Mrs. Kennedy. And you, too, Mr. Kennedy." Carol stepped forward and hugged Ruth Kennedy as she entered the house. She could only imagine how sick at heart they were, but both managed a weak smile. Trying to keep their spirits up, she thought. It wouldn't be easy.

"I'm sure Ruth told you we have been expecting this," Henry said. "Please come on in and have a seat."

"Thank you. I'm so sorry that I couldn't give you better news, but our search of the ravine put a sad end to our hopeful expectation. And yours."

"Would you care for some tea?" Ruth asked. Carol wasn't interested in tea, but decided that 'yes' would be more appropriate. The Kennedys should be given the chance to be busy, to do whatever they needed to do to maintain a normal life. Or at least to try to.

"I suppose I don't really want to hear the details," Henry said, "but I've always believed that it's better to face the truth. So why don't you tell me what happened to Martin."

"I can only tell you what I know, and there are still things I don't know. But Martin had fallen into the ravine on the Slocomb property. How or when we don't know yet. It's a deep ravine, and he'd fallen quite a distance. A specialist I know well, a good man, will do what he can to provide answers to our questions. But right now all I can say is that he died in that ravine."

"I take it that you don't know what caused his death. I mean whether he died from the fall or was dead before he fell."

So, the Kennedys, like Carol, had considered that their son's death might have been caused by someone else, perhaps even Slocomb. She wanted to be able to say that this was impossible, but that would not be true. Better to be honest but try not to encourage the Kennedys to think their son had been murdered.

"I know that this is unbearably hard for you. We'll do what we can, as fast as we can, to determine what happened. The sad thing is that Martin is gone, and you will do your best to accept that. But I'm sure he'll be very much in your memories."

"Ruth and I may disagree about this," Henry said, looking at his wife, hoping that there would be no disagreement. "But I really want to know how he died. If Mr. Slocomb had anything to do with it, he should pay for what he did. It's not that I believe in revenge, if you know what I mean. But taking a life, especially if you do it because you hate people who are different than you are, can't be tolerated. Or shouldn't be tolerated. I never thought I'd feel like this, but discovering that Mr. Slocomb is one of those people who keep on fighting the Civil War and probably wishes the Klan was still alive changed my mind."

He started to sound angry, but caught himself.

"I'm sorry, sheriff. It's possible that I'm being unfair to the man. Martin never said bad things about him. But that awful Nazi poster - I guess it got to us, made me think he could have been responsible for Martin's disappearance. Do you think he could have killed Martin?"

"I try not to make judgments about people until I have more facts," Carol said. She also deliberately avoided using the word 'autopsy.' It had a way of conjuring up pictures that upset members of the family. "I'll know more within a week."

"Do you plan to have a church service for Martin?" she asked, changing the subject.

"We should. It's a tradition. Of course there wouldn't be many there. We attend the Southport Baptist Church, and I expect to talk with Reverend Shattuck about it."

"I wasn't urging you to have a service, but it sounds like a good idea. I'd like to be there. In fact, there should be a fair number of local people who'd want to attend."

"I'm afraid you're wrong about that, sheriff. We're new here, and there aren't many of us - many African Americans, that is, around the lake."

"A service for Martin is open to everyone, and I think there are many of our neighbors who would want to come. I grew up here and have worked here for many years, and I believe that Mr. Slocomb does not represent our Crooked Lake population."

"Well, we'll have a service anyway if Reverend Shattuck can schedule it."

"Good. Please let me know when it will be. I'll be there, as will several of my officers. And others." Carol chose not to share with the Kennedys her plan to take the initiative to fill the pews.

When she left the Kennedys, Carol was wondering how they would cope with the loss of their son. He had given them nearly fifteen years of what must have been a hard life, with challenges that had eventually brought them to Crooked Lake. And then they had made a decision which she was sure would haunt them the rest of their lives. Whether Adolph Slocomb was responsible for Martin's death or not, he would almost certainly give them sleepless nights and bad dreams. She felt sorry for them, and hoped that their loss would not cause them to abandon the lake and return to the south.

She and Kevin had planned to go out for dinner, but she no longer felt like it.

CHAPTER 36

It was the third day in Mrs. Kimbrough's house. Clemens had a different view of the situation. He saw it as the third day under Mrs. Kimbrough's thumb, for she had found an excuse for visiting him, unannounced, every day. She always had an excuse, but he was convinced that she was simply looking in on him to make sure that he was keeping his room in immaculate shape, something he had never done in every place he had lived. He debated with himself whether he should tell her to respect his privacy, but suspected that it was an argument he couldn't win. Better to give her a few days; maybe she would cease intruding if he made a small effort to make his bed, use the waste basket for its intended purpose.

His plan to become a town handyman had gone nowhere. Of course it had only been three days, and only one of those days since his announcement of the service had gone up in downtown North Forester. He had actually been lucky that he had been approached by one local resident. The problem was that what he had been asked to do, open a clogged drain, had taken all of five minutes and could have been done by the homeowner if he had had a plunger. He'd give his plan a week or two to take off; if it didn't, he try something else. What he didn't know.

Clemens' initial dislike of North Forester had only become more frustrating. It wasn't just Sarah Kimbrough's unwillingness to leave him alone and the likelihood that he would never make much money as a repairman that bothered him. What troubled him most was that the small town and its dull population seemed unlikely to give him an opportunity to participate in some action that would serve his strong view that white people were losing their dominant role in the American society, while blacks and an endless tide of Hispanic immigrants were getting ever larger handouts from the country's spineless government. The last time he had had the opportunity to protest this process was when he had lived in Virginia. Unfortunately, his white rage there had produced a result which had forced him to move to New York. And events beyond his control there had necessitated yet another move. He was still in New York, but he was in no place where he could take to the streets and fight for a cause he believed in. He pounded his fist on the arm on his chair. It was the closest he could come to doing anything except accepting the fact that he had to agree that for the time being he was on the losing side of the battle for control of the American dream.

For a moment or two Clemens let his mind concentrate on the situation back on Crooked Lake. It briefly focussed on the hogs. He thought about them often. There was a time when he had felt badly that they could be dying for lack of food. He wondered if he should have asked Hopkins to feed them, or, better yet, to find someone to take them. But that would let more people know what he was doing, and while he believed that Hopkins shared his views on the racial issue, he wasn't entirely sure, not sure enough to involve him in taking care of the hogs he had left behind. As time went on, he found himself worrying less about the hogs; they would have died anyway, thanks to his knife and the public's taste for spareribs.

Better to think about the sheriff. She would be trying to figure out where he was. At least for awhile, and then she would have to accept the fact that she would never know. That would make two sheriffs he had fooled: the one he had never met in Virginia, and the one he had spent altogether too much time with on Crooked Lake. Neither knew or would know that he was now in a tiny town east of the Hudson River. Eventually, and she hoped soon, both would have closed the books on him and he would be free to find a new place to live where it wouldn't matter if he participated in another rumble on behalf of the white race.

He wasn't much of a TV watcher. He turned the set on frequently, but didn't have the patience to watch half an hour of anything, much less an hour or two. There had been a time when he had checked the news to find out what had become of the Virginia conflict between the white protestors and the nasty counter-protestors. Now that conflict was old news, and he hadn't seen his name mentioned in nearly two years. But he was bored, thanks to the somnolence of North Forester, so he turned on the TV. It was a news channel that came on, and to his surprise it was in the middle of a report of another conflict between white suprema-cists and their liberal opponents, this one in Colorado. He sat back down in his chair to watch it, but was immediately turned off by the fact that it seemed to have been poorly attended and that the announcer was obviously supportive of the liberal, multi-racial counter-protestors.

"What a joke," he said aloud. "We haven't got any guts any more. Just putting up with those damned hybrids!"

For the first time since he had come north to avoid a possible jail term in Virginia, Kenneth Clemens found himself thinking about whether he might - or should - stop running away and resume what had been his more active (and more satisfactory) political life. Was he still serious that this was a white country, that it was necessary to openly challenge its 'takeover' by multi-racial scum? Why had he become a coward? Why had he gone into hiding in a shack in nowhere and then in a miserable small town, also in nowhere? Why had he stopped communicating with old friends who were more courageous?

He turned the TV off. He knew the answer to the questions he was asking himself. He wasn't a coward. No, but he was smart enough to know that he would be hurting, not helping, his cause if he was stupid enough to spend time in jail. He could hate the fact that the cause to which he was committed was not going any-where very fast, but in the long run it would win. And he would be around to see it prevail. In the meanwhile, he had made a dif-ference, forcing two incompetent advocates for so-called law and order to waste their time and money pursuing him. He'd put up with North Forester and Sarah Kimbrough for a little longer - well, maybe quite a bit longer - and enjoy the successes he had already scored.

CHAPTER 37

The dry summer gave way to three days of rain, hard pounding rain that raised the level of the lake and spoiled the vacations of many renters. Carol had considered driving to North Forester to see if by some chance Slocomb was there. But the weather discouraged the trip, the weather and the poor odds that it would help her investigation. She actually spent some of her time dealing with issues that had nothing whatsoever to do with the Kennedy case. Nothing that is but Doc Crawford's autopsy.

She reached Doc on her second call.

"Have I wasted your time?" she asked.

"Depends on what you mean by wasting my time. I was going to call you this afternoon, but was holding off until I had a chance to review it one more time. Fact is that as of right now I can't say I've found any convincing evidence that the boy was killed by somebody before he went down the ravine. He certainly wasn't poisoned. Nor shot or knifed. If he was dead before he went over the edge of the cliff and down to the tree where you found him, it would be because someone beat him with something like a strong tree limb. That's possible, but I'd be irresponsible if I said that's what happened. His head and upper body took quite a beating, but I saw nothing that couldn't have come from the trees and bushes he encountered as he fell. Let's put it this way. The man you *think* may have killed the boy may have done it, but if he goes to trial and has a good attorney he'll be able to make a good case that it wasn't him. And unless someone saw him push the boy into the gorge, I suspect you'd have to find some other way to get a conviction."

"I guess this is what I expected."

"This is one of those situations where autopsies aren't quite as conclusive as we like to think they are."

"I understand. Just keep me informed if you find anything that makes you more certain, one way or another."

"Of course. It sounds like an unpleasant case. Sorry."

Having turned her attention once more to Slocomb, if unsuccessfully, Carol decided to take another trip to his former dwelling on the hill. Not that she expected to find anything of importance that she had missed earlier, but she was now thinking about Doc's reference to a tree limb. She had never looked for a limb, at the house, in the field between house and the ravine, or elsewhere in the vicinity. Besides, it was a new day and the rain had finally stopped, so she might as well scout the area of Slocomb's former home one more time.

"I'm making another trip to the Slocomb house," she told JoAnne. "Don't mention it to Sam unless he sounds like he really needs to see me. He thinks I'm obsessed with this case."

"Maybe he's right," said JoAnne with a laugh.

The trip to Slocomb's former residence on the hill was now thoroughly familiar to Carol and took her less time that it used to. She intended to examine the surrounding fields for anything that might have been used to knock out or even kill Martin Kennedy, but her first order of business was the house itself. She had gone through it earlier, but realized that she had only been getting a better picture of Slocomb's living space, inasmuch as she had never seen more than the living room on previous visits. That he was still gone was apparent the minute she turned onto the long drive from the road to the hog pen. No sign of the truck. An empty porch. The absence of noise.

Carol circled the pen, putting more distance between herself and the bad odor that always came from Slocomb's hogs, the hogs he had left behind. She knew the front door was unlocked, and there was no reason to announce her presence. Once inside, she immediately smelled the stench that she remembered from her last visit, the stench that came from the kitchen and the remains of the hog Slocomb had killed and cut up before leaving. It wasn't only the smell that reminded her that Slocomb was slovenly. He had made no effort to clean up anywhere, bedroom and bathroom included. This time, however, Carol commenced a more thorough search of each room and its cupboards and drawers than she had when last in the house. Whatever else he had been, Slocomb was not a hoarder. She found nothing that seemed superfluous, except, that is, for an empty water bottle. She remembered it from before. This time she took it from the kitchen cabinet where it lay in the back, behind a well worn Revere pot which Slocomb had presumably used to cook his simple suppers. What prompted her to remove it from the cupboard, she realized, was that it reminded her of something she had seen somewhere.

Carol held it up to the light and tried to recall where she had seen one like it. As was often the case, her memory served her well. It was a bottle that cyclists carried on their bikes. She probably had seen one like it on JoAnne's bike, which her trusty aide always parked in her office. But what was such a bottle doing in Slocomb's kitchen? When she had asked him if Ernie Eakins had paid him a visit while on the Gravel Grinder, he had said no, that he didn't know what a Gravel Grinder was. But her initial interest in the water bottle faded quickly. Many people kept water bottles, not only bike riders. Slocomb could easily have kept one with him for hot weather work on his property. Yet the one in her hands was identical to the one on JoAnne's bike, identical in size and shape, in color. In any event, she'd take it back to the office and ask JoAnne for a comparison. No point in making assumptions about something as common as a water bottle.

The only other item she found which she had missed or forgotten from her last visit was a small tube of vaseline. Instead of being in the bathroom, it was in the kitchen cabinet to the left of the sink. She looked at it carefully, decided that it had no purpose of importance to her investigation, and put it back next to a cereal box which no longer had fresh milk to go with it. Which left only one place in or near the house which she had not examined, the hog pen. She had ignored it earlier because it was filthy and she had no interest in dirtying a fresh uniform. She might ignore the open pen where she had seen the hogs lying and rolling around, but there was no reason for not examining the room into which they disappeared occasionally within the pen. What it was for, Carol didn't know. Did they sleep there at night? Was it where they went to escape mid-day heat? Maybe it was where Slocomb kept bags of food for them. She'd find out.

She returned to the porch, where she again caught the smell of the pen. It was simply disgusting. Would she have to make her way through the muddy slop in the pen to get into the mini-barn? She hoped not, but made her way around the pen, looking for an entrance which was at least marginally cleaner. Suddenly she came to an abrupt stop. There, to her left behind the sturdy fence, was a sight that came close to causing her to throw up. The hogs were there. So was the mud which had been created by days of heavy rain and the digging into the muck by the hogs. But more important than the hogs and the mud was a human body, surrounded by flies, and obviously dead.

It had obviously been buried in the dirt floor of the pen, and might have remained buried had it not been for the steady downpour and the frantic digging of the hogs, who by now had gone several days without anything to eat. The body showed clear signs of having been eaten by the hogs. Carol didn't know it for a fact, but she had heard that hogs were omnivorous. She had assumed that this was the case for wild boars, but what she was looking at in the pen convinced her that domesticated hogs were also omnivorous, if not all the time at least when they were starving.

Not only had Slocomb's hogs found food, they had found Ernie Eakins. She was unable to be absolutely certain that the body was that of Eakins. It was covered with mud and its face was still buried in the muck. It definitely wasn't Martin Kennedy, whose body had already been found in the ravine. She had never expected to find the missing cyclist on Slocomb's property, certainly not in his hog pen. But this was certainly a cyclist, dressed like one with a cyclist's helmet beside him where it had been knocked off by the hogs. From where she stood she couldn't swear it was Eakins. But who else could it be?

Carol wanted to enter the pen and examine the body more carefully. But she was reluctant to do so. For all she knew, the hogs could be dangerous. Whether they were or not, she didn't have the strength to push them out of the way so she could get a better look at what she assumed to be what was left of Eakins. In any event, she would be trying to maintain her footing in the slippery mud. The prospect of doing so did not look promising. The more she thought about it, the more it looked like a job for her male officers. Or better yet, for a local farmer who raised pigs and knew how to handle them. That, of course, posed a problem. She would have to bring somebody into the case who knew nothing about it, at a critical time when an outsider's presence was not a good idea. She decided to call Sam.

Still staring at the dreadful sight across the fence, she buzzed her deputy sheriff.

"Bridges here," he responded.

"It's Carol, and I have a problem. Actually I have made a very shocking discovery. Where are you right now?"

"Yates Center. What's the problem?"

"Are you with someone, or can you drop what you're doing and come over to where Slocomb lived before he flew the coop?"

"Give me ten minutes and I'll be on my way. Do I have to wait until I join you or can you give me a head's up now?"

"I was taking another look, trying to see if maybe I'd missed something over here. I didn't exactly miss it - it's something that came to light after all the rain that we've had in recent days. It's in the hog pen, and it's a body, a dead male body that's been buried there. I'm sure it's the cyclist who never came back from the Gravel Grinder, Ernie Eakins. An ugly sight, covered with mud and partially eaten by those damned hogs. I can't haul it out of the quagmire; you can't either. But between us maybe we can decide what to do. I need your help. Okay?"

"My God, what next? You never talked about Slocomb killing Eakins. Kennedy, yes, but not the bike rider. This is going to be a big one, isn't it? I'll be there as fast as I can. Do you want me to pick up Parsons or one of the other men? Sounds like we should leave Dockery out of this one."

"It's not a pretty sight for any of us, men included. But no, just bring yourself. Do you remember how to get here?"

"It's where Damoth broke his arm, right?"

"That's it. And hurry."

When his car pulled up, Sam was out of it quickly and at the sheriff's side, peering over the fence at the hogs and the body, still muddy but largely out of the dirt.

"I never thought I'd see something like this," he said. "You sure it's Eakins?"

"Ninety nine percent sure. I can't imagine that Slocomb has been going around disposing of locals he doesn't like. But the bike race or whatever it was, went up this way, or close. The question is why would he have killed the cyclist. Young Kennedy is problem enough. Hard to believe Slocomb hired him so he could kill him. Maybe he didn't. It could have been an accident, given what we know. But if this is Eakins we're looking at, and I'm virtually sure it is, his being buried in the pen is no accident. Which means Slocomb killed him. But why? He's white, not African-American, not Hispanic, not somebody from a culture Slocomb despises."

"And Slocomb isn't here anymore so you can question him, not that he'd answer your questions. He probably cut out and ran so you couldn't find him and ask about the guy with the bike."

"When he left town there was no evidence anybody was buried in the pen, and frankly I would never have guessed somebody was.

So what questions would I be asking? I'll bet he thought Eakins would never be found. And probably he wouldn't have been if it hadn't been for all the rain we've had, practically an invitation to the hogs to dig deeper."

"If that's what he was thinking, he'd be pretty dumb. We do get storms around here, as he must know, and unfed hogs do get hungry and go searching for their dinner."

"True, but maybe Slocomb was in a hurry and not thinking about the long run. Who knows? But we've got to do something. Can't leave the body down there in the muck, especially with all those hogs still in the pen. Let me be honest, Sam. I thought about going in there and bringing him out. But I don't know anything about hogs, or pigs for that matter. Maybe they're dangerous. Besides, I'm not up to fighting with big animals for possession of a human body. And I'm not even talking about wearing a coat of mud. What do you suggest?"

"In the first place, you made the right decision. Not going into the pen, I mean. Heaven knows what would have happened. But you're right. We've got to get him out of there. I suggest we get ahold of a farmer, somebody who knows something about creatures like that. Hopefully, there's a farmer around here who has a pig or two. He'd probably have some of the stuff you feed them with, or at least would know what you'd use and where to get it. With luck, we'd get a crew together, like we finally did to get that kid out of the ravine, and then we'd remove Eakins."

"I take it you don't know any pig farmer."

"No I don't. But I'd suggest we contact Barrett."

"Barrett? He's not with us anymore. You know that."

"Of course I do, but I remember shooting the breeze with him when he was, and he lived - probably still does - in farm country out on Preemption Road. Seems to me he had a friend who kept pigs and maybe goats. Could be wrong, but that's a place to start. Let me give it a try."

"Go ahead, do it. I'm not anxious to spread this all around the lake, but we'll have to risk it. I'll talk to the guys that run the meat departments around here. We have to move fast."

So Carol and Sam got busy searching for help in the hog pen. Carol also alerted the coroner. By that evening they had arranged, thanks largely to ex-officer Barrett, that the Cumberland County Sheriff's Department would take steps the next day to turn the Kennedy case into the Kennedy-Eakins case.

CHAPTER 38

"Hi, it's me," Carol said as she walked in the back door. "And wait until you hear my news of the day!"

Before he had a chance to give her a welcome home kiss, much less ask what her news was, the phone rang.

"I'll get it," he said, stopping at the kitchen phone. "Hello, Kevin Whitman here. You want me or the sheriff? She just walked in."

He looked at his wife, his smile disappearing.

"It's Bridges. And of course he wants you, not me. Tell him you're tied up all evening."

"Hello, Sam. What have you learned?" She listened for a couple of minutes, shook her head, and waved Kevin away when he used his soft voice to ask whether she would have to turn around and leave for the evening. "Sounds good. Thanks for thinking of Barrett. Why don't you and I take two cars. That way I can stick around longer than you'll need to. Ten okay? See you there."

"What's that all about? You're not going out, I hope."

"No, and I never expected to. Sam and I are planning the morning. Tomorrow morning. Let me change and I'll fill you in."

Kevin, who was used to Carol being called out for some emergency or other, relaxed and removed a bottle of Chardonnay from the fridge.

"Now, pour me one and I'll tell you how the plot thickens," Carol said as she returned, minus her uniform and her gun.

"This is a story that goes better with wine, is that it?" Kevin asked.

"They all do, this one better than most. Except that it's slightly gruesome."

"Gruesome? What that supposed to mean?"

"Let me begin at he beginning. Back at the old Slocomb house, where I'd gone to see if I'd missed anything. Which I had, something big and shocking. Well, that's not entirely true. I didn't miss it. The heavy rain exposed it. In Slocomb's hog pen. There, lying in the mud, was a dead man, and unless I'm wrong it's Ernie Eakins, the missing cyclist."

"Eakins in the hog pen? What on earth - wait a minute! You're telling me that that no good guy who'd gotten rid of the African-American boy also got rid of the Gravel Grinder rider?"

"That's what it looks like. And you'd be just as shocked as I was to see this muddied remains of a man down there with a few hogs. Worse, from the other side of the fence it looked as if the hogs had been eating him."

"Hogs eating a human being?" Now Kevin sounded shocked.

"That's what it looked like. I was't going into the pen to be sure. Neither was Sam."

"Give me a couple of minutes," Kevin said as he got up and headed for the study. "I want to google the diet of pigs. I've always thought of them like cows and sheep, and cows and sheep sure don't eat people. Why should a hog?"

"I seem to be be wrong, but I didn't think so either. In any event, what matters isn't what hogs eat but that somebody had been buried in Slocomb's hog pen."

Three minutes later Kevin returned from the study.

"You're right, unless google is wrong. Our porcine friends are known to chow down on humans, not every day but occasionally. What is it that you and Bridges are going to be doing about it tomorrow?"

"We'll be innocent bystanders. We've latched on to a neighbor of Jim Barrett's. Remember him? Good officer who traded in his uniform for an environmental job. Anyway, he knows a man who raises pigs and thinks he can help us solve our problem. At least he knows something about the animals Slocomb left behind when he pulled *his* vanishing act."

"So you'll be watching Eakins being brought out of the muddy pen and then bundling what's left of him into an ambulance for a trip to the morgue."

"That's abut it, assuming everything goes right."

"I'd suggest you and Sam wear your winter galoshes, just in case."

"Thanks for the advice."

"By the way, you've said nothing about a bike," Kevin said. "If, as you seem to think, Eakins is Slocomb's victim, he'd have a bike with him. Did you see one in the hog pen?"

"No, and thanks for bringing it up. My mind was so fixed on his body that I forgot about his bike. It could still be there, buried deeper. But that seems unlikely. So where is it? It's possible that the bike gave out on him and he walked to Slocomb's. If so, the bike could be somewhere on the roadside before he reached Slocomb's and he went there to get help. But I've driven the route Reiger says is the one the Gravel Grinder took. Several times in fact. And I never saw a bike."

"If I'd been Eakins, I'd have walked the bike to Slocomb's place, not left it on the roadside. But I'm not Eakins, and maybe the guy in the pen isn't Eakins either, which means that maybe you can forget about a bike. Or -" another thought came to Kevin - "maybe it was Eakins and he did leave the bike behind and somebody stole it."

Not for the first time, Carol was amazed with the way that Kevin quickly came up with possible explanations for problems, one after another.

"We're talking about Eakins, I'm sure of that. Which means that we have to account for his bike. And let's assume that his bike wasn't buried much deeper and that it wasn't stolen. Big assumptions, but we have to start somewhere. So while you're brainstorming, give some more thought to where Eakins might have left his bike."

"Okay. You say you've been poking around, looking for evidence against Slocomb. And you found nothing in the house. How about the shed at the hog pen? I know you didn't jump over the fence to where the hogs and what we guess is Eakins' body were. But you haven't mentioned the shed. The bike could be in there, although Slocomb probably has more intelligence than to leave it there. Then there's the ravine. Maybe he threw it down there like he did young Kennedy? That's two options."

"I'll examine the shed tomorrow. The ravine is a better possibility, but Slocomb's smarter than that, too. He'd know we'd search the ravine for Kennedy, and if we can find him we could find the bike."

CHAPTER 39

The team which gathered at the hog pen the next morning included Johnny Morris, Jim Barrett's neighbor, Morris's two sons, Frank Kubiak, an old friend of Morris's, Sam Bridges and Carol Kelleher from the sheriff's department, the county coroner and an ambulance with its crew. Barrett would like to have been present, but he'd been given an assignment which he couldn't miss. Carol explained the problem, but it didn't need much explaining. Morris seemed confident that he'd be able to handle the hogs and remove the dead body, and what happened in the next half hour proved that he knew what he was talking about. The only decision that Carol had to make was whether to use a hose to clean the mud from the body which had been extricated from the pen. She chose to do so, using a lengthy hose that was coiled up near the porch. The mud gone, Carol was now sure that she was looking at what was left of Eakins, even if she had never seen him.

Taking advantage of her role as the person in charge of the morning's unusual task, Carol had asked the Morrises to dig a deeper hole where Eakins had been buried. The dirt had been replaced, but Carol was now convinced that no bicycle had been buried with the body. The hogs had meanwhile been given something more appropriate than a dead human to eat and had been allowed to return to the open pen.

"Many thanks for your help," Carol said as the Morrises and Kubiak prepared to leave. "As I'm sure Jim Barrett told you, the county will pay you generously for doing what Officer Bridges and I didn't have to do. And almost surely couldn't have done. Nasty job, but it had to be done. It's pretty obvious that what you've been doing is related to a crime. It would be better if word of this isn't spread all over upstate New York. I'm sure you'd love to share the morning's adventure with friends and neighbors, but I suspect you won't be surprised if I ask you not to do that, at least not until I say it's okay. You understand my problem, don't you?"

"Of course. You heard the sheriff," he said to his sons. "This is our secret for the time being. Anyway, I'm glad to be of help. And you're right. It was an adventure."

Carol shook hands (dirty hands) and thanked Morris once more, telling him she knew whom to call if she had another 'hog crisis' to worry about.

It was now possible to examine the inner room of the hog's shed. As she had expected, it contained no bicycle. Which meant that the bike Eakins had been riding was not going to be found on Slocomb's property. Where was it?

"Sam," she said, as they headed back for their cars, "we've found Eakins but, believe it or not, I feel worse, not better. Now I've got the problem of having his wife view the body. The very thought makes me sick."

"Thank goodness, that's what sheriffs have to do, not deputies."

"Thanks for your help. But back to the bike. Eakins would probably be on Slocomb's property not because he'd lost his way but because something happened to his bike while he was nearby. Maybe the bike wasn't ridable, so he left it where he had the problem, on the roadside, and walked to the nearest house, and it turned out to be this one. Why don't we get in my car and check out the road that goes by here, see if there's a bike somewhere close."

"But we've been on the road that goes by his place. Twice. Today and the other day when Damoth broke his arm in the ravine. Don't you think we'd have seen a bike?"

"But the stretch of the road we've been on is the one coming up the hill to where we are. Suppose he had his problem after he passed Slocomb's? Let's say within a mile or two further up the hill. Maybe even further. Cyclists tend to be in good shape, and they value their bikes. So a long walk would be possible if it was neces-sary."

Sam looked doubtful.

"Could be, I guess. But why wouldn't he walk his bike back to Slocomb's, not leave it on the roadside?"

"No idea. Maybe the bike's problem made walking it difficult. Don't ask me what I mean; I don't own a bike. Anyway, it won't take long to check out the hill. Chances are we won't find a bike. It's still possible that Slocomb hid it somewhere we haven't thought of. Come on. We're close, it'll only take a few minutes. You drive, I'll look for bikes."

They bumped down the rutted road from Slocomb's until they reached the almost equally bad road that ran up the hill.

"I took this road when I was tracing the Gravel Grinder with Joe Reiger," Carol said. "But according to him this wasn't where the Gravel Grinder went. It went off to the left about a mile back down the hill. We didn't know, of course, whether Eakins had made a mistake; we were only looking for places where he might have. Now I want you to turn right. That puts us on the road Eakins would have been on if he had a bike problem and had to go back to get help. I'm guessing that that's what Eakins would have done whether he walked the bike to Slocomb's or left it by the roadside. You following me? It's complicated."

"I'm with you," Sam said as he turned and headed up the hill road.

"Okay, now let's slow down. If there's a bike ahead, we don't want to miss it."

Ten minutes later, Carol suggested that they call it a day.

"We've come - what does the odometer say, four miles?"

"Almost five."

"I think we can forget this excursion. There's been no sign of the bike. Eakins wouldn't have come anything like this far, I'm reasonably sure. Which presumably means that Slocomb is cleverer than I thought he was and has done something that makes finding the bike pretty close to impossible."

"Do you need to find Eakins' bike to make a case in court?"

"It would help, but I think what we found in the hog pen will do the trick. The downside of that, of course, is what it will do to Connie Eakins."

CHAPTER 40

Carol had just decided that it wasn't worth spending more time searching for Ernie Eakins' bike when an unexpected phone call brought the bike back to her attention.

She and Bridges had taken their own cars and returned to the sheriff's office in Cumberland, both happy to be away, at least temporarily, from the hog pen. JoAnne appeared at Carol's office door almost as soon as the sheriff had settled into her chair and begun to go through the items in her in-basket.

"It's another call about the Kennedy/Eakins case," she said, having gotten into the habit of using the shorthand title Carol had initiated. Sometime ago Carol had begun to regret coining the expression.

"Who's this one from?" She hoped it wasn't Connie Eakins, much as she could sympathize with the woman who had almost certainly lost her husband.

"No one I ever heard of. A police chief in Horseheads." JoAnne laughed. "How'd you like to live in a town with a name like that?"

"What's his name and what's he calling about?"

JoAnne stopped laughing. Obviously her boss didn't share her view that Horseheads was a funny name for a town. At least not today.

"He said he was George Jacobs, but he didn't tell me what his call was about. Except that it had something to do with Mr. Eakins."

Suddenly Carol was very interested in the call from Horseheads.

"Call him back, let him know I'm here."

It took about five minutes for Jacobs to drop what he was doing and get to the phone.

"You're the sheriff in Cumberland County, right?" was his opening line. Interested as she was in the call, Carol was mildly annoyed by the question. Who did he expect to be on the line?

"Yes, I'm Sheriff Kelleher. What can I do for you, Mr. Jacobs?"

"First, let me tell you that I'm not sure you're the person I need to talk to. B. J. Shirk gave me your name. Or should I say your role as the sheriff in the county west of us. Do you know him?"

"I'm afraid not. Who is Shirk?"

"He lives here, or near here, and he drops by occasionally to see me. We go back quite a few years, back to high school."

"Like I said, I don't know him. Or you, I'm sorry to say, although we're in the same business. What does this man Shirk want you to pass on to me?"

"Like I said, maybe I should be speaking to someone else, but I'm sure you'll let me know if you don't know what I'm talking about. Anyway, it really isn't terribly important, more of a lost and found call. One of our citizens came by the other day and said his son had found a bicycle in a field near one of our county roads not far from where he was playing catch with a friend. The boy seemed to think it was a 'finders, keepers' situation, but his father told him the bike belonged to whoever had left it in the field, assuming we could find him. There was a metal plate on the bike with the name of Ernie Eakins. I took the bike and put it in a cupboard at police headquarters, then placed a notice in the local paper and forgot about the matter. Forgot, that is, until my friend Shirk stopped by."

"So does your friend Shirk know Eakins?"

"No. In fact I don't think he knows anything about him, but he's one of those people who reads practically every line in the local paper about property sales, thefts, lost and found items, you know, that kind of stuff. Anyhow, he'd apparently come across something awhile back about a Finger Lakes bike race over on Crooked Lake where one of the cyclists got lost. But he also read on the lost and found page our notice about a lost bike that belonged to somebody named Eakins, and it reminded him of the bike race story. It seems your name as the investigating officer had been mentioned, and he passed it on to me. Are you investigating that bike race?"

"Not the race so much as the missing rider, Eakins." Carol had told Sam that she was no longer much interested in the missing bicycle, but it was no longer true. She had no idea how the bike had gotten to Horseheads, but Eakins' cycle was apparently in a police locker there. "Tell me about the bike. You said it had a plate which identified it as belonging to Eakins. What else can you tell me about it? Is it damaged, and if so how? What's the name of the family - the boy and his dad - that brought it in? Has anybody called or stopped by to see if it could be theirs? Oh, and what color is it? I'll be talking to the wife of the man who owns it, and I'll want to describe it to her. In fact, we'll want to come over to your police department just as soon as we can and pick up the bike."

"You haven't discovered Mr. Eakins, I take it?"

"Not yet." There was no need to tell the Horseheads policeman that he was almost certainly in a morgue in Yates Center. "Please, try to answer my questions - is the bike damaged, the name of the man who turned it in, any questions from people who've read the newspaper notice. This may help me find Mr. Eakins. At least I hope it does."

"Well, the bike looks to be in good shape, probably pretty expensive. And no, nobody has answered the lost bike notice. Oh, the man who brought it in. Name's Rizzo. Can't recall his son's name, only that his father wouldn't let him keep the bike he'd found. Poor kid, must have thought he'd been really lucky."

"As it happens, I won't be the one to pick up the bike. My deputy, Officer Sam Bridges, will do it. This afternoon. The Rizzo kid may not have been lucky, but I am, thanks to you. And to this guy Shirk. Fifteen minutes ago I had just about given up on the missing bike. You've made my day."

After hanging up, Carol hurried down the hall, where she caught Sam just before he was ready to hit the road again.

"We've found Eakins' bike!" she said.

"How did you do that?" Sam was obviously surprised.

"The police chief down in Horseheads has it. He just called to report that some kid found it in a field. Now you're going to go and collect it."

"I thought you'd decided that we didn't need it."

"That was because we couldn't find it. Now we face a different problem. How'd it get to Horseheads? The minute the police chief told me he had Eakins' bike I thought of his wife worrying that maybe he was having an affair with another woman and had gone to see her. But that's a non-starter, as I realized immediately. How could he be buried in a Crooked Lake hog pen and then travel to Horseheads to be with someone other than Connie. I can't tell her he's alive, but I can tell her he wasn't cheating on his marriage."

"I know what you mean, not that it'll make her happy. But I'd be careful. You don't know that he honored his marriage vows."

"I know, but it'll be easier to finesse his marital misadventures, if there were any, than to avoid telling her that he was buried with a pack of ravenous hogs."

"Okay, I'd better check my car's gas gauge and set off for Horseheads."

"Have a nice trip," Carol said, and went back to her office to spend some time pondering how and why Eakins had gotten into

Adolph Slocomb's hog pen while his bike had travelled another seventy miles to Horseheads.

CHAPTER 41

The memorial service for Martin Kennedy drew a large crowd. Several attendees commented that they had never been to one so large, and it was the opinion of many, including members of almost every denomination, that the service was impressive and ecumenically tasteful. Carol, who had done much to fill the church through her conversations with community leaders, was grateful and sure that the Kennedys' sorrow would have been eased somewhat by this generous outpouring of support.

She had spoken briefly with Ruth and Henry after the service, but she decided to visit them again at their home, Kevin at her side, that evening. Before she did so, however, she had another, much less pleasant thing to do, something she had somewhat irresponsibly postponed while she tried to decide how to do it. Connie Eakins had to be told of her husband's death. Mrs Eakins no longer believed that Ernie was alive. Nor was it likely that she any longer thought that he might have run off with another woman. None the less, official word that he had been killed and buried in what might be called a farm east of Crooked Lake would come as a shock. What would be a greater shock was that he had been buried in a hog pen and partly eaten by those hogs.

But it had to be done. Carol placed the call to the Eakins' residence as soon as she got back to the office. She had learned that a sister had moved in temporarily to provide support to her beleaguered sibling, but fortunately Connie herself answered the phone.

"Mrs. Eakins, this is the sheriff. Both of us have been sure that I'd be making this call, sooner or later. Well, I'm afraid I'm doing it now. We have found your husband. I'm sorry to report that he's dead, and probably has been since the day of the Gravel Grinder bike event. His body was buried on a hill property above the east shore of the lake, and it is the former owner of that property who was responsible."

"I'm not surprised to hear this, sheriff, although you will know that I'm deeply saddened. The fact that it's taken so long to learn what happened made it clear to me some time ago that he must be dead. I regret that I momentarily had the feeling that perhaps he had gone off with another woman. But in retrospect that was stupid of me and absolutely not fair to Ernie. Do I dare to ask what happened on him?"

"Of course, and what I tell you is going to be hard to hear. He was almost certainly killed by the man who owned the property on which he was buried. We don't know why he did it, but it seems to have something to do with the fact that your husband visited him because he was having trouble with his bike and that they had an argument that ended with Ernie's death. I am so sorry that I have to tell you this."

"It's funny, but I'm not all that surprised by what you're telling me. Ernie was much too good a cycle rider to have had an accidental death. But to be killed and to be perfectly innocent, that's horrible. Have you caught the man who did it?"

"Not yet. He left the lake, probably right after what he did and before we found your husband's body. Finding him and bringing him to trial is now my office's number one priority."

"Where is Ernie's body?"

Now comes the hardest part, Carol thought.

"It's in the morgue, but I would much rather you not see him. Sometimes it's much better to remember what our loved ones looked like when they were alive and we were happy than how they look in death. Do you understand?"

"I understand what you are saying, but I can't imagine that I'll never see him again."

"Just give us a little time," Carol said. She wasn't sure what she could do with that time to make a visit to the morgue or to a funeral establishment desirable.

There was little more to be said. Connie had taken the news about as well as could be expected, but Carol was glad that Mrs. Eakins had her sister with her. She hoped that they had a close and warm relationship.

The Kennedys' tragedy was just as sad and traumatic, but they had had more time to deal with it, including the memorial service. Nonetheless, she wasn't looking forward to her trip to their home in Southport. Kevin's presence at her side would help. She picked him up at the cottage at a quarter to five.

"We won't bother you for more than a few minutes," she said when they arrived, "but I wanted to introduce my husband and tell you again what a beautiful service it was."

"Thank you so much, sheriff, and don't feel you have to rush off," said Ruth. "Henry and I will probably need lots of company in the days ahead. I must say, the number of people attending the service was both a surprise and a thoughtful reminder of how nice our neighbors are."

She paused and then asked a question.

"Do I dare ask if you had something to do with how many people came? Most of them were strangers to us. And, as you know, there aren't many of us here on Crooked Lake. African-Americans, I mean."

"Please don't blame me. I did say something to a few people I know, but I'm sure the church was filled by people who could put themselves in your shoes and wanted you to know that."

"In any event, thank you. It isn't as important as burying Martin, but I have to ask if you've discovered anything which ties Mr. Slocomb to Martin's death, or any success in finding him?" It was Henry Kennedy who asked the question.

"I'm afraid not." Doc Crawford still did not know whether Martin had been killed before he disappeared in the ravine, and doubted that he'd be able to prove that he had. "Almost everybody at the service knew Martin had fallen into a ravine, but they knew little or nothing about Slocomb. I didn't think it was my place in the circumstances to talk about him. You can, of course, if you want to, but my job isn't to spread rumors or complicate your life if I don't have to. And no to your other question. Unfortunately, I don't know where Slocomb is. I'm still searching."

Rarely does a memorial service leave its participants in an upbeat mood. This one was an exception. Carol had hoped that Martin Kennedy's would be well attended and do something to lift the spirits of his grieving parents. It might not last, but for a day at least the community had come together and made her proud. Unfortunately, the service had not succeeded in dispelling the harm which Adolph Slocomb had brought to Crooked Lake. Harm which most of those at the service still knew nothing about.

Ironically, the person who was perhaps least happy about the situation at the lake was Slocomb himself, partly because he was no longer there but mostly because he had begun to worry about whether the things he had done to reestablish white supremacy in the United States were no longer safely behind him. He had made his way out of Virginia, changed his name, and escaped from punishment of the murder of a counter protester. Living above Crooked Lake in New York's Finger Lakes for two years without any sign that Virginia authorities knew where he was had given him a strong sense of security. Then he had once again taken to the road to escape from his own foolishness, moving to the Massachusetts border, adopting another new name, and taking up residence in a wretched small town that, while boring, seemed safe enough.

But now Slocomb, with another new name, Clemens, was losing his sense that all was well, that he had effectively separated himself from his past life. Not from his values, of course, but from what he had done to give life to those values. He had always taken it for granted that the first amendment to the constitution protected his right to believe what he wanted to believe and to speak his mind about those beliefs. He had even been amused that the ACLU, which he regarded as a disgusting liberal organization, supported his right to speak openly and forcefully, to champion what others called hate speech.

Now, several weeks into his unhappy residence in North Forester, he no longer felt safe. He wasn't sleeping well. Some nights he hardly slept at all. His days were spent walking around, driving around, and no matter where he walked to or drove to he couldn't shake a feeling of anxiety. While he was trying to shake off his anxiety, he was occasionally repairing things for stupid people who should have been able to take care of the problem themselves. He hated the Kimbrough woman, who never let him forget that she was better than he was. He hated his former friend, Frank Walker, who had argued that as a good Christian he should love his enemies, not kill them. He hated the Crooked Lake sheriff, who, like Kimbrough, wouldn't leave him alone. As he drove up to the house on Crown Street on returning from a trip to Pittsfield, a trip which had done nothing to relieve his anxiety, he deliberately blew the truck horn at two women on the sidewalk to his right. There was no reason to do it except that it made him feel momentarily better when the startled women moved quickly further away from the road.

"Out of my way, you bitches," he said under his breath.

What's the matter with me? he asked himself. The women weren't black. They weren't in his path; they were minding their own business. I must be more careful, not become someone who's talked about as an unpleasant trouble maker. I have to be seen as a quiet newcomer, a good neighbor. But how am I to play the good neighbor? I have never been a good neighbor. I've never even been close to the other men who share my commitment to the white cause.

Clemens let himself into his room and made his way to the bathroom mirror. What he saw was what he had seen day after day for most of his life, an ordinary man who had never made an effort to improve his appearance. What mattered was what was going on around him, and what was going on around him was the gradual decline of rules that favored people like him. White men still dominated many fields, including Wall Street of course. But too many, for all practical purposes, were relegated to what he thought of as white trash, pushed to the sidelines by increasingly large numbers of people who were black and brown, who spoke no English or bad English, who -

"How many times have I rehearsed this speech," he asked the man in the mirror. "I'm a broken record. I'm going nowhere."

He knew why he was anxious: he was in North Forester. On the surface it was a safe haven because no one there knew anything about what he had done in Virginia or Crooked Lake. But that was also a problem. The people who knew what he had done, or who were conducting investigations into what he had done, were not in North Forester. They were in the communities where he had been and which he had left in his search for personal safety. The one he was most concerned about was on Crooked Lake, the tenacious sheriff.

The odds of her finding him should have been very low, so low as to make it virtually impossible. So why was he so anxious? The answer was that he had made a phone call to his only friend on Crooked Lake. The friend's name was Burt Hopkins.

Hopkins had been the manager of the meat market at one of the stores he sold pork to, and Hopkins knew that he had hurriedly left town, leaving most of his hogs behind. Slocomb, now Clemens, had considered making the call ever since arriving in North Forester, and finally had done so in hope that he'd learn what had happened to the hogs and, more importantly, whether his departure had stimulated any local gossip. He had been careful, never mentioning where he was calling from or sharing any information which

Hopkins, accidentally or intentionally, might pass on to anyone else.

It was the night after his call to Hopkins that something came to mind which shattered his sense of security. It had to do with the question that had come to mind when he was in South Williamsport, debating where to make his next home after leaving Crooked Lake. One of the options was North Forester. He had tried to remember who had told him about it, why the name had come to mind at that moment. He couldn't remember, but decided it didn't matter. He'd go to North Forester. He hadn't told Hopkins where he was living, of course, but as he went over his conversation with the manager of the meat market that night it occurred to him that he had made a note of the name of the town. When he'd done it he didn't know, or where it was he didn't know. After all, It was a relatively long time ago.

But something told him it might be important. He got out of bed and went to the file in which he had kept data on his pork sales. It took him only three minutes to scan the papers in the file.

There was no reference to North Forester on any of them. Had he thrown anything out? Had he left something behind in the hill top house? Suddenly Kenneth Clemens was worried. What if that nosy sheriff had rummaged through the belongings which he had not taken with him? What if she had found a reference to North Forester? What if she had inferred that he might have gone there when he left Crooked Lake? It was unlikely that any of these things had happened. He had always seen her as tenacious but not too smart. But what if he were wrong? He didn't know her, didn't really want to know her. Maybe that was a mistake.

In any event, Kenneth Clemens was now anxious. In fact, his anxiety was so strong and so persistent that he found himself spending almost all of his time worrying about what to do to keep Sheriff Kelleher from finding him, where ever he was.

CHAPTER 42

"So, finally I get to meet one of those Cumberland County officials who have to deal with murder all the time." The Horseheads police chief smiled as he shook Sam Bridges' hand. "Just kidding, of course. We're really jealous."

"I'll bet you are," Sam said. "Truth is, day in and day out we spend most of our time playing poker."

"Then why I am I turning this bike over to you?"

"Ah, yes, the bike." Sam eyed the locker. Its door was open, and there was the cycle they had been looking for ever since Ernie Eakins had not returned from the Gravel Grinder. "Not bad looking, is it? Fairly new. Thanks for taking care of it. Now we'll see if we can figure out how it came to Horseheads. The guy who rode it never came this far, nor as far as I know did any of the other riders."

"You want to see where the bike was found?"

"I can't see why that's necessary. My trunk has too much stuff in it, so if you'll give me a hand I'll put it in the back seat and let you go back to catching *your* murderers."

"Haven't had one in more than a decade. Just can't keep up with you."

It only took a couple of minutes and Sam was on his way back to Crooked Lake, with a prearranged stop at *Quinton's Bike Shop* in West Branch.

"Well, here I am," Sam said to the owner of he shop. "You ready to tell me what's wrong with the bike, why Eakins had to leave the Gravel Grinder?"

"Looks like it will be easy," Quinton said. "No obvious sign of trouble, but then I didn't expect one. Ernie took care of his bikes. Just give Sean here and me a few minutes and I'll tell you what the problem is. Or was."

Sam wasn't sure Quinton would be able to find the bike problem in a few minutes, but he chose to stay at the shop rather than leave the bike and head back to his office for what was left of the afternoon.

Less than ten minutes later Quinton announced his intention to take Eakins' bike for a ride on the road to Yates Center, suggesting that he was about ready to report on its condition. Sam put down the newspaper he'd been reading and stepped outside to watch as Quinton's set off on his trial run. It was barely twenty minutes later that he returned.

"I went almost all the way to downtown Yates Center, and if there's something wrong with the bike I'm damned if I know what it is. Rides like a charm. Either Ernie fixed it himself or there was never any problem."

"The sheriff's going to be upset," Sam said. "Well, not upset, just surprised. It seemed pretty obvious that Eakins left the Gravel Grinder track because something was wrong with his bike. Now you tell me that's not the case."

"All I'm telling you is that the bike is in good shape. Nothing wrong, and I think I know a few things about bikes. But -" Quinton paused, looked at the bike, and turned back to Bridges. "When you picked up the bike, did it have water bottles in its cages?"

"Its cages? I'm not sure what a bike cage is, but there weren't any water bottles."

"Here," Quinton said, taking hold of the place where a bike rider would have stored the bottle of water he would drink on a hot afternoon. There were two cages, both empty.

"These were empty? Did you ask the cop in Horseheads if they'd removed the water bottles?"

"No. Why would they do that?"

"Maybe to take a drink," Quinton said.

"That's crazy. There was one of those water dispensers right there in the chief's office. Why strip the bike?"

"You're probably right. But if you are, it suggests that Ernie left the Gravel Grinder track because he needed a drink and didn't have any water." But Quinton quickly changed his mind. "But that makes no sense. Nobody, certainly not Ernie, sets off on a long ride like that one with no water bottles on his bike."

"Maybe he'd already drunk all the water he'd brought with him."

"What kind of experienced biker would be that foolish? Anyway, there aren't any bottles on the bike. It could be that they'd fallen off, jarred loose on a rough, unpaved road, like the one the Gravel Grinder takes."

Sam shrugged. His trip to Horseheads was beginning to look like a waste of time.

"Yeah," Quinton added. "It's possible. I remember a time I lost my water bottle. Kicked myself for my carelessness."

"So this is the best we'll be doing today," Bridges said. "I should learn not to be optimistic."

Back at headquarters, Sam gave Carol a quick summary of where they stood: bike fine, water bottles missing.

"That may not be the whole story," Carol said. "There's a water bottle in Slocomb's old place. It may be one of the two Eakins had on his bike; then again it may not. But considering what Quinton had to say about losing those bottles on rough roads, maybe we should search the road that leads up the hill to where Eakins must have peeled off for his fatal side trip to Slocomb's. It'll take two of us, one to drive and one to look for bottles on the roadside or in the ditch. You up to another day of this?"

"Yes, assuming I can reschedule my annual physical."

"Go ahead and see your doctor. I'll dragoon Kevin into coming along."

CHAPTER 43

"Am I driving or riding shotgun?" Kevin asked as they finished breakfast.

"It probably doesn't matter. But I think I'll drive, inasmuch as I know the road better than you do. Which means that you've got to keep your eyes on the roadside. Wide open! It would be easy to miss a colored bottle in the weeds and brush in the ditch. The county doesn't do much of a mowing job along these back roads."

"What do you think the odds are that we'll find something?"

"Oh, we'll find something. More likely that it'll be a dead wood-chuck than a bike bottle."

Carol picked a familiar intersection as their starting point, a place where she was sure Eakins would already have begun drinking water as he rode.

Kevin told her to stop three times in the first twenty minutes, but the closest they came to a water bottle was an empty beer can.

"Why is it that human beings insist on littering our highways?" Carol asked after their third stop unearthed a child's broken doll.

"It gives us neat environmentalists something to complain about," Kevin replied, as he added the doll to a sack in the back seat.

"How close are we to Slocomb's?"

"No more than three, four miles. I wasn't very optimistic." Carol said.

"Me either. Then what?"

"I wish I had a plan B, but - wait a minute, what's that?" Carol slowed down. "There, next to that crown vetch."

She stopped the car and Kevin got out to poke around in the weeds to which his wife had given a name he'd never heard of.

"You're right. There's a bottle here. How'd you see it? That was my job."

"Does it look like a water bottle?"

"I guess so. You can put water in anything."

He handed it to Carol.

"I think we may be in luck. This looks exactly like one I saw in Slocomb's kitchen cabinet. What's more, it's full of water. See?" She unscrewed the top and poured some out. "Want to know what happened? Eakins had finished the other bottle, lost this one due to the rough road, and went up to Slocomb's to get a refill of the other one. Case closed."

"Wait a minute. What do you mean, case closed? You don't know that this bottle belonged to Eakins. And even if it did, you don't know for sure if Slocomb killed him, much less why he did it. How does finding a dime-a-dozen water bottle on a crummy back-woods road prove anything?"

"Okay, I know the case isn't closed. I'm just celebrating a minor victory. A few minutes ago I was sure we'd come up empty, and now we know why Eakins went to Slocomb's. And that I'm sure of. Well, ninety percent sure. There's a lot I don't know, but let me take credit for what I do know. And for spotting the bottle!"

"How'd you do that?"

"Just chance - I thought I saw a glint of color. I was lucky. Now, let's go on to Slocomb's and pick up the other bottle. Then we'll see if they fit the cages on Ernie's bike."

CHAPTER 44

Carol had been feeling good most of the day about finding the water bottle. It pretty much guaranteed that Eakins had visited Slocomb's for the purpose of refilling his one remaining solution to dehydration. But as evening approached, her enthusiasm had begun to wane. The reason for his being at Slocomb's was important, to be sure, but why had it resulted in his death? It was possible that he had had a heart attack, and that Slocomb, in a panic, had buried him in the hog pen. But why would he do that, when it would make more sense and be much easier to call somebody in authority and report what had happened to the cyclist? The answer, quite obviously, was that he was afraid that he wouldn't be believed. Carol was quite sure that she wouldn't have believed such a story. No, Slocomb had killed Eakins. When she first raised the question of whether a cyclist had paid him a visit, he had claimed that he didn't know anything about a bicycle event and that he had seen no cyclist on his property. It was clear that he had thought about it and decided what he would do if asked about seeing Eakins, or any other biker for that matter. Just to be sure she would ask Doc Crawford to perform a second autopsy. And she knew that he would not find that death was due to a heart attack.

By the time she left the office and headed for the cottage, she had become completely frustrated with her inability to come up with a reason why Slocomb would have killed Ernie Eakins, a white man who didn't buy his pork, whom he had never met, and who had a simple and unthreatening explanation for coming to his door.

"I'm home," she called out as she entered the kitchen. "I hope you're in a mood to play sleuth with me. I need some help."

"What? Again? I thought I'd already been a big help this morning," Kevin said as he came out of his study. "I was going to tell you about my progress on the computer. It's been very cooperative today. I'm even trying to work a water bottle into the plot."

""A water bottle in an opera article? You must be desperate. Well, so am I, and I *do* need your help. You do the honors with the wine, and I'll ditch this uniform. I'm not sure I deserve to be wearing it."

"I thought it was a good day. What went wrong?"

"Give me a few minutes and I'll tell you." She vanished into the bedroom, leaving her puzzled husband uncorking the Chardonnay.

"Okay," Carol said as she took her favorite chair on the deck. "I haven't lost my mind, so you can relax. The problem isn't what happened to Mr. Eakins or the water bottles on his bike. We know that. But you know me, always worrying about the next problem, and in this case the next problem is driving me crazy. It isn't new. It's been on my mind for some time - well, at least since we found Eakins' body in the hog pen. I'm sure you know what's on my mind: why did Slocomb kill Eakins? We know he thinks white men are losing control of the country and that something has to be done about it. But Eakins is white. He may not be a protestor on behalf of white supremacy, but neither are millions of other Americans. There must be scores of people like him who engage in protests, but I can't remember reading about one who killed another white man because he didn't join a white rage march. So why did Slocomb do it?"

"This is the problem I'm supposed to solve?"

"Of course not. I'm just asking you to join me in a brainstorming session to see if we can come up with some reasons which might explain why he did it. Right now I'm stumped."

"Does it matter? I mean, if he killed a man, and I accept your view that he did, isn't that enough to have him on trial for murder?"

"To me it matters. Let's treat it as an intellectual puzzle. It's like every case we read about where somebody shoots someone and then the media spend days speculating as to why he did it? The shooter always has a motive. Slocomb surely had a motive. What was it?"

Kevin promised to think about it, and Carol challenged him to think about it now.

"Okay," Kevin suggested, "how about Eakins saying something that irritated Slocomb."

"But what? You don't kill someone who complains about a bad odor or your taste in furnishings. What might Eakins have said that made Slocomb that mad?"

"Suppose our cyclist saw the Nazi poster and criticized it?"

"The Kennedys saw it and criticized it, and they weren't killed."

"No, but their son was."

"We don't know that. Maybe he did fall into the ravine, like Slocomb says."

"But what if Eakins got annoyed with Slocomb - let's say for refusing to fill his water bottle or telling him to get off his property. Maybe he even expressed his belief in white rule, his hostility to a multicultural society. Eakins took offense, and the next thing you know they were in an argument that ended in a fatal fight. That's possible, given what you've told me about the hog man."

"I can't imagine that Eakins, anxious to get some tap water and rejoin the Gravel Grinder, would have wasted his time in a stupid argument that would cost him his life."

"You asked me to come up with ideas that might explain Eakins' death." Kevin sounded as if he'd lost his interest in the discussion.

Carol's expression changed. Something had occurred to her.

"You're right, I did, and I've just had another idea. We've only been talking about Eakins. What if we added the Kennedys' son to the discussion? What if he was in the room, and became involved in the conversation. Or the conversation turned away from filling Eakins' bottle and to young Kennedy. I'm not sure where I'm going with this, but it occurs to me that Eakins and Slocomb might suddenly be talking about Martin. Do you get my point?"

"I think so, and if you're right I can imagine an argument, maybe a more violent one."

"Exactly," Carol agreed. "I never met Ernie Eakins, or discussed his political and cultural views with his wife or his friends. But let's assume that he wasn't, like Slocomb, a white racist. After all, people with views like that are, thank heaven, a decided minority in the US. So what if Eakins heard, even saw, something - conflict, say, between Slocomb and Martin Kennedy - that disturbed him. Suppose he was truly upset about it, about what he thought of as mistreatment of the black boy with down's syndrome, and said so. Suppose he even threatened to report it to whatever local officials handle such complaints. Don't you think that Slocomb could be so riled that he'd do something about it?"

Kevin was obviously intrigued by Carol's suggestion.

"And do something because he feared that Eakins was in a position to uncover a life he'd been trying to hide. Now that could be a motive for murder, couldn't it?"

"Yes it could, but I can't see how I can prove it, even if it's true. Nobody saw what happened at Slocomb's that day except Slocomb himself. The others are dead. If I could find Slocomb, it's hypothetically possible that I could get him to confess what he did to Eakins. But I can't imagine he'd do anything but laugh at me. Besides, we're only speculating about why he killed Eakins, and speculation isn't a promising court strategy."

"So where does that leave us? You asked me to speculate as to why Slocomb killed Eakins. Now what?"

"Maybe it's time to take a trip to North Forester," Carol said without enthusiasm.

"Why North Forester?"

"Because it's the only lead I have as to where Slocomb might be. It's probably a wild goose chase, but what choice do I have? Besides, I don't think I'll be the one to take that trip. He knows me, and I don't have any convincing disguises."

"What about me?" Kevin asked.

CHAPTER 45

The next day Carol called Doc Crawford and convinced him that he would probably be doing a second autopsy. Her next task was to do what she could to find out whether Adolph Slocomb had recently moved to North Forester.

Her problem was that while she knew Slocomb and could very probably recognize him in that small village, he also knew her and could make himself scarce. None of her officers had ever met him, and it was doubtful that she would be able to describe or sketch him well enough to make him recognizable to any of them. The same was true of Kevin. The alternative, at least initially, was to phone people in North Forester who might know enough about the village to tell her whether a recent newcomer who might be Slocomb had settled there. From what Byrnes had told her, the size of the village made it likely that anyone she called would be aware of newcomers. But how could she be sure that whoever she called wouldn't mention it to others, making it likely that Slocomb would be warned that it was time to pull up stakes again? She could try the police or real estate agents, but she wouldn't know them and hence wouldn't know how they would respond to her request that they say nothing about her call. She had grown up in the Finger Lakes and knew all too well that there were few secrets in small towns.

In the end she decided that she'd run the risk by driving to North Forester herself. The chances that Slocomb was even there were not great. And she would not wear her uniform or drive an official car. She might even change her hair-do and otherwise do what she could to add a few years to her age. Having decided this much, Carol had Tommy Byrnes do what he could to identify people she should talk with. The result was a small list.

Kevin urged her to be careful and kissed her good-bye early the next morning. It was a boring drive. North Forester proved to be a boring village. Carol stayed in the car as much as she could, casing what might be called the business district and the residential neighborhoods. She had an uninspired lunch in an uninspiring eating place with only a few diners, being careful to draw down over her forehead a dated cloche hat that had been her mother's.

The name at the top of Tommy's list had been Earl Sargent, a real estate agent (and, according to Tommy, the only one in North Forester). When she saw his sign, Carol hesitated and then decided that she would have to take a chance on Sargent's word not to tell people about her visit and her questions. She'd try to sound innocent.

"Mr. Sargent, glad to find you here. I won't take much time. I'm not in the market for a house, but I work for an upstate company that needs some statistical information for a study on population mobility in this region." Needless to say, her presence at his door had nothing to do with population mobility or a non-existent study. "Do you mind if I come in and ask a few questions? As I said, I'll be brief."

The real estate agent looked confused, but welcomed her into his office.

"Population mobility? Like people coming and going? Not much of either around here. Newcomers are rare, and long term residents typically stay until they die. I don't know what the current figure is, but I'm sure we have fewer citizens living here than we did when I was born."

"I'm here because I thought maybe a real estate agent like you would be a good source for data on the study I'm involved in. North Forester doesn't seem to have any industry. Is it a nice place where people who work in some neighboring community sleep - you know, live while they work in some busier nearby town, an exurb you might say?"

"An exurb? North Forester?" Sargent looked like he might laugh. "Hardly. We're a sleepy place all right, but our business is mostly doing things for each other, like feeding us, gassing up our cars, supplying what we need to function from day to day. We're small town America."

"In the typical year, about how many old timers move out, new-comers move in?"

"You want firm figures?"

"As close as you can be. This is just a first round; we're trying to get a rough picture of the area, but I'm sure I'll be back later, or one of my colleagues will." Carol didn't like what she was doing. Better to get down to her real mission.

"Let's start with newcomers. Any new residents recently?"

"It's been a slow year. A couple from the Bronx came here back in February, bought an old house and began to modernize it, then got cold feet and left in May. Very sad for them and for us. Then a guy came here just a few weeks ago, but he ended up as a renter from a woman who'd lost her husband recently. That's about it. Last year wasn't great, but it was better."

"So it adds up to one newcomer this year, discounting the cou-ple who changed their minds. Any idea what the man who settled for a rented room - or was it a whole floor - wanted? Short term, I'd imagine."

"I think so, but I'm not sure. Don't see much of him, although he has put up notices that he's available for repair work. Otherwise he seems to stay out of sight."

"Maybe I should talk to him. Do you remember his name?"

"Not entirely sure, but I think it's Clemens."

Carol was debating with herself what more to ask. It was obvious either that Slocomb had not come to North Forester or had changed his name and was the renter of space in some widow's home. That seemed unlikely, knowing what she did about Slocomb's need for privacy. But it was a possibility, and she'd have to follow up. Hopefully she could get by with some information of where the rented property was located. She decided to risk it.

"It's on Crown Street, corner of Shaker Boulevard. The woman who rents a room is named Kimbrough. She'e a piece of work, as you'll find out."

"Thanks. I'll be going now, and I do wish that North Forester's luck takes a turn for the better soon. A negative economy is tough for any community, and I'm sure it's tough for you personally."

Carol turned the door handle and started to leave when she spotted a pick-up truck moving slowly down the street in front of the real estate agency. She immediately realized she'd seen it before, not only once but many times; a banged up right rear bumper and its mottled grey color gave it away. It was Adolph Slocomb's. He couldn't have been doing more than five or six miles per hour. Why? Maybe her imagination was working overtime, but it took but a second or two to guess that Slocomb had noticed the car in Sargent's lot. Could he be in the habit of watching the lot, which in this troubled small town must be empty most of the time, worried that the police could be looking for him? That she had figured out that he was in North Forester? She had driven her personal car today, but Slocomb would be smart enough to know that she would not be driving a police car.

The truck sped up, the driver having seen the agency door open. There was no longer any reason for her to visit Kimbrough. Slocomb had obviously settled in North Forester. There was no point in her tailing him. She hadn't come with the purpose of arresting him and taking him back to Crooked Lake, but only to find out if he had moved to North Forester. He had. What's more, she couldn't try to arrest him without support, and Bridges and her other officers were at the moment miles away in Cumberland County.

She doubted that Slocomb knew that she was in town. He had no idea that she drove a blue Ford when she wasn't in her official car. Of course he could come back and ask Sargent whom he had been talking to, and the agent would tell him that it was a woman doing a study of population mobility. If asked to describe her, she had no idea what Sargent would say. She hoped he would say that she looked middle aged, around fifty. There was nothing she could do about it if he said forty. In any event, he would not say she was a sheriff.

Carol was now in an interesting position. She knew that Slocomb lived in this small town. She even knew in what house he lived. The advantage was hers. But she could not visit the house on Crown Street, slap him in handcuffs, and drive him back to Crooked Lake. She needed help. One thing she could do was drive back to her office, do what had to be done to make the arrest, and return to North Forester, this time with Bridges and perhaps another of her officers with her. But that would take time, time which a nervous Slocomb might use to take to the road again. Alternatively, she could stay where she was, assuming she could find a motel, and call Sam with instructions and an order to meet her in North Forester a.s.a.p. This way she would be able to keep an eye on Slocomb and avoid two long drives and the loss of more time.

Another drive around town made it clear that North Forester had no motel, a sure sign that it was really a dying community. Perhaps that was why Slocomb had chosen it. Carol had no intention of sleeping in her Ford, and she knew that she wouldn't be able to stay awake until Bridges arrived. Oh, the hell with it. Why would Slocomb move because he had seen an old Ford in a real estate agent's parking lot? Why had she let this nasty hog farmer become such a frustrating obsession? The answer, of course, was because he was not just a nasty hog farmer. He was almost certainly the murderer of a man who enjoyed bike riding and probably of a young African-American boy with down's syndrome.

She'd find a motel, and she'd call Bridges.

CHAPTER 46

When Carol's alarm clock awakened her the following morning in the nearest motel, it took her but a few minutes to recall the plans she had made with Sam the day before. He and Parsons would arrive today, ready to arrest Slocomb (or Clemens if they were the same person) and take him back to the jail in Cumberland where he would stay until she had done what had to be done either to try him locally or arrange for his rendition to Virginia. She had no doubt that Sheriff Prescott in Blacksburg would agree to the latter. After all, the crime which had led to this unusual summer had occurred at a march by white supremacists in his jurisdiction. She had no proof that the man who had killed a counter protestor in Virginia was the same man who had hired Martin Kennedy and killed and buried Ernie Eakins in a hog pen on Crooked Lake. Their names were different. But she was almost certain that Prescott's Decker was her Slocomb, and with Sam's help she expected to prove it once they had met the man in the house on Crown Street.

The breakfast nook at her motel only served coffee, orange juice, and stale muffins, but she had agreed to meet her colleagues in the motel rather than in North Forester. She was finishing her second cup of coffee when Officer Bridges walked through the door, accompanied by Officers Parsons and Byrnes.

"Well, well. Looks like we're going to have our squad meeting here rather than in Cumberland."

"I know, but I did some highway math and figured we might need another driver for Slocomb's pick-up."

"That's me," Byrnes said. "But first, how about hitting the breakfast bar. I'm starved, not to mention exhausted."

"He's not exhausted. Slept most of the way over." Sam enjoyed ribbing his partner.

"That's okay," Carol said. "I'm sure all three of you are bushed. Night time driving is never much fun, especially when you're coming this far."

Sam was the one who had offered to make the trip to the Hudson Valley that night. They'd take turns at the wheel, he said, and the traffic on the thruway had been lighter than it would have been the next day. And so four members of the Cumberland County Sheriff's Department had themselves a welcome breakfast with two cups of coffee each.

Carol had no idea what Slocomb (or Clemens) did with his days. There wasn't much to do in North Forester, so it was possible that he slept a lot when he wasn't engaged in the repair jobs he had apparently undertaken to pay Mrs. Kimbrough. This guess proved to be a good one, and fortunate for the sheriff's team. It was only 8:10 when Sam's Chevy reached the turn onto Crown Street. To their right, against the curb in front of the house Sargent had said now housed both Kimbrough and Clemens, was Slocomb's old pick-up. He had either taken a walk or was still in his room, and perhaps in his bed.

"Let's not park here," Carol said. "How about down the road, past several houses. You two stay in the car. Sam, you come with me and we'll try the landlady's door. I'm sure it's the one on the porch, between those big windows. If she's in - at this hour I'm assuming that she will be - she's going to surprise her renter by letting us into his digs."

"Do you expect trouble?" Parsons asked.

"I have no idea what he will do, but the fact that the pick-up's still here means we've got him." I hope so, she added silently.

The door bell rang three times. The third ring was answered.

"Yes?" The woman who opened the door didn't look pleased to be bothered so early.

"I assume I'm talking with Mrs. Kimbrough," Carol said. "I know I don't look like a sheriff, but I am. The name is Kelleher. This is my colleague, Sam Bridges. We'd like to step in."

"Did somebody report me?" she said, backing away from the door and letting them in.

"No, this isn't about you. We're here because we have to talk to the man who is renting from you. Clemens, I believe his name is. I'm assuming that at this hour he's still in his apartment. We didn't want to go barging in without talking with you first."

"Is he a thief or something?"

"I'll be able to tell you more after we speak with him, but we believe he's running away from the law. And that means from us. Our jurisdiction is west of here, over in the Finger Lakes. Both my colleague and I would normally be wearing our uniforms, but I'm reasonably sure that Mr. Clemens would have disappeared by now if he saw law officers on the streets of your town."

"You're telling me that a criminal is renting a room from me?" Kimbrough no longer looked annoyed. She looked scared.

"That is why we're here, and I'm going to ask you to let us into Mr. Clemens' apartment. You're in no danger. Just do what I ask you to do."

It had occurred to Carol that Mrs. Kimbrough might have suspected that she and Sam were themselves thieves or even worse criminals. But without their uniforms they wouldn't appear to be carrying guns, and Carol had tried to avoid language which would frighten the woman. She hoped that Mrs. Kimbrough wouldn't panic.

"Now, when you open the door, just say 'these people would like to see you' and step aside. Don't tell him whom we are or what we want. We'll take care of that. If you'd like to go back to your part of the house, that's okay. In fact, it would probably be a good idea. Two more of my officers are in a car further down the street, and they'll be joining us. Remember, we are all members of the sheriff's office in Cumberland County."

"But Mr. Clemens owes me some money," Kimbrough said. This issue hadn't occurred to Carol.

"No problem. We'll see that you're paid whatever he owes you." What was it that the real estate agent had said about Clemens? That he made money doing repair work? He was now his own Martin Kennedy. Assuming he was in fact Adolph Slocomb.

Mrs. Kimbrough followed orders. She unlocked the door to Clemens' rental room and stood aside as Carol and Sam pushed into the room. As she had hoped, its occupant was still in bed, but rising up on an elbow as he reacted to the noise.

"What's going on?" he shouted. "Who are you?"

He hadn't had time to move his legs out of the bed when he recognized the sheriff. And it was at that same moment that Sam spotted the man's wallet on the bedside table. Sam was quicker, beating Clemens to it.

"This is my room! " he shouted. "Now get out. And give me my wallet. I'm not going to let a couple of goons march into my space and pretend they have a right to do it. Out, damn you, or I'll call the police."

"We are the police, Mr. Slocomb," Carol said, "and you are the one who's in trouble. Big trouble. Now that you're awake, I'd appreciate it if you'd get dressed. Officer Bridges will stay with you, just in case you think you can make a run for it. I'll step outside out of respect for your privacy."

Carol did step outside, where a nervous Mrs. Kimbrough was still standing. Following plans they had discussed earlier, she waved at Parsons and Byrnes, who quickly made their way to the house on the corner.

"What's the word?" Tommy asked.

"He's Adolph Slocomb, a man who has lived on Crooked Lake for the last year or two and whom I have talked to many times. The chase is over."

"Carol, come here," Bridges called out from the bedroom, where he was holding Slocomb, still in his pajamas.

She stepped inside, only to be greeted by Slocomb's angry voice as he tried to free himself from Sam's tight grip.

"You don't have any decency, do you, sheriff? How'd you like it if I came barging into your bedroom when you were undressed? So get out and take this gorilla with you!"

Sam pushed Slocomb onto the bed and pulled the blanket over him.

"There. That better?" Sam said. At that moment Parsons and Byrnes walked in.

"Need some help?" Parsons asked.

"I'm sure the sight of the four of us will prevent any stupid behavior. Don't you think so, Slocomb? Or should I call you Clemens, or maybe Decker? Here," he said, turning to Carol. "Look at this."

Carol took the wallet with its three folders. She didn't need to study them; Sam had just told her what they meant.

"I think your days as a murdering white supremacist are over," she said to Slocomb.

"That's what you think. You can't prove a damn thing."

This wasn't the time to have an argument with the angry man in his pajamas. He had committed murder on Crooked Lake and, before that, in Virginia. The only issue yet to be decided was where Decker/Slocomb/Clemens would be tried.

"Excuse me," Carol said. "I'll join Mrs. Kimbrough outside so you can dress without us women in the room. My colleagues will help you if you need their help. Then it's on with the hand cuffs and we're off for the lake, which I'm sure you've been missing. Oh, I almost forgot. We'll make a thruway stop for breakfast. Can't afford to ruin your day."

CHAPTER 47

The caravan pulled into Cumberland several hours later. Carol drove her own car, Bridges his car with Parsons and their angry but for the most part silent prisoner in the back seat, and Byrnes in the pick-up truck.

"Welcome home," Carol said to the man she would always think of as Slocomb as Sam and Officer Parsons helped him out of the back seat and up to the second floor sheriff's office. "Sorry we can't provide you with a bigger, neater cell, but I'm sure you'll manage."

Slocomb, now surely Decker, had chosen not to play games with the sheriff. According to Sam he had lapsed into a surly silence most of the way back to Crooked Lake. He knows, Carol decided, that trying to one up me every time I taunt him is not a good strategy.

He knows I'm aware that he is really Michael Decker. But he doesn't know that, thanks to Sheriff Prescott, I'm aware that he killed a counter protester in Virginia. Of course he also knows that Ernie Eakins is dead and that Eakins' body has been discovered in his old hog pen. He may still think I don't have a persuasive case against him for what happened to Eakins, but I doubt he still believes I'm making a fool of myself by arresting him. We'll see.

"Welcome home." Kevin gave Carol a big hug. "I was afraid you'd be tied up longer over in North something."

"I might have been there longer if Sam hadn't chosen to drive all night. I've got a team of workaholics, don't you know? More important, Slocomb was there. We caught him in bed, sleeping late. Now he's in our lock-up over in Cumberland."

"Can't believe it. I'm married to the fastest sheriff in the west. Did he put up a fight?"

"The advantage was mine. I had Sam plus Parsons and Byrnes with me. Needless to say, it wasn't his finest hour. He threatened to call the police, but I reminded him that we were the police. According to Sam he clammed up practically all the way back. I assume that he spent the trip planning what he's going to do. I know that that's what I was doing. I'm bushed, but I'd like to share with you what I think should come next. You ready?"

"Of course, I am. And needless to say, I'm surprised that you've wrapped up the case so fast."

"The case isn't quite wrapped up yet, as you'll see. But we're in the home stretch. And the way I see it, the man who's behind bars at the moment, my friend Adolph Slocomb, isn't the one who's going to pay for his crimes. It's Michael Decker."

"Wait a minute. You've been telling me you finally arrested Slocomb, but now it's Decker who's the guilty party. Two and two don't equal five, Carol."

"No, of course not. But remember our conversation about the battle down in Virginia between the white supremacist protestors and their more rational adversaries? The one where a guy whose white rage got out of hand and he slammed somebody's head into the pavement? It was awhile ago, but the sheriff down there called me and brought me up to date. Remember?"

"Vaguely. Didn't the man go into a coma and then die? But what about -"

Then he remembered.

"The man who killed him was named Decker, and Decker ran off to Crooked Lake and became Slocomb. Right?"

"You've got it. One man, two murders, maybe three if it turns out that young Kennedy didn't just fall into the ravine."

"How did you discover that Decker and Slocomb were the same man?"

"Because Slocomb, whatever we choose to call him, made the mistake of carrying data for three men in his wallet: Decker, Slocomb, and his current North Forester name, Clemens. Not very smart."

"I suppose if you're going to change your name every so often it helps to have those names handy. Otherwise you'd lose track of who you're supposed to be."

"Whatever the reason, Decker basically gave his game away. My problem now is to decide what to do with the information he gave me."

"I'm not sure I'm following you. You've got him in your cell in Cumberland. Why not go ahead and put him on trial?"

"For what?"

"For killing Eakins. Maybe Kennedy, too."

"Would that it were so easy," Carol said.

"Okay. Forget Kennedy. Maybe he did tumble into the ravine without Slocomb's help. But Eakins, he's a slam dunk, isn't he? Those hogs didn't bury him in their play pen."

Carol had already given a lot of thought to this one.

"You've never read Joseph Caldwell's novels, have you?"

"No I haven't, but so what?"

"Why don't you try him? More specifically, I'd recommend one titled *The Pig Did It*."

Kevin looked as if Carol were having fun at his expense.

"Come on, Carol, we're having a serious discussion. The pigs didn't do it."

"Of course they didn't do it. But if you want a few laughs, try that book. But what if we were to try Slocomb for the death of Eakins, and he found himself a clever lawyer who argued that the cyclist had some kind of seizure and dropped dead on Slocomb's property. What would Slocomb have done? He could have buried Eakins where he expected he wouldn't be found, giving his lawyer an opportunity to hand him an alibi."

"But I thought Doc Crawford was going to do an autopsy that would rule out a heart attack and might even provide evidence that Eakins had been beaten to death."

"But Crawford is frank about the fact that autopsies are frequently less conclusive than we like to think they are. And Eakins would have spent quite a bit of time with the hogs. A jury has to be convinced that what the prosecution is arguing is the truth beyond reasonable doubt. Sure, we've got a good case, but it just might be harder to prove."

"Harder than what?" Kevin asked.

"Harder than the Virginia case. Now we know that Slocomb is really Decker, and that Decker is the man who killed a man in that demonstration down in Virginia. How's a clever defense lawyer going to finesse that fact? Which brings me around to what I think I'm going to do. Why bring Decker to trial up here when we could send him back to Virginia and let Sheriff Prescott handle the case against him? Prescott says that the photo taken at the demonstration is not some fuzzy 'maybe that's him' shot. He's confident that Decker was the killer, which means that if I can prove that Slocomb (and Clemens, for that matter) is Decker, a trial for murder in Virginia is more certain to end with a conviction than one on Crooked Lake."

"Can prisoners be transferred like that?"

"They can and often are. It's called interstate extradition, and I'm pretty sure New York and Virginia could work something out. I'd have to talk with Sheriff Prescott, not to mention people in my jurisdiction who have authority, but I can't imagine that it couldn't be done."

"So you'd be willing not to take credit for bringing the racist to trial and convicting him?"

"Why not, if it makes it more likely that he's put away? But I have another reason for letting him be tried in Blacksburg. If he's tried here for Eakins' death, the trial will inevitably be dealing with issues that will be terribly painful for both Mrs. Eakins and the Kennedys. Just put yourself in the courtroom, listening to sick, even nauseating, details of what happened or is alleged to have happened to members of your family, to your friends. It would be cruel, don't you think?"

"Yes, I agree. But you aren't going to be able to avoid telling Connie about it forever, or the Kennedys either."

"That's true, and I dread doing it. But if the trial is in Virginia, and concerns Decker, I'll be able to do it one on one, without everyone on Crooked Lake watching and listening to all the details. I'll be able to pick the time and the place, and I'll be speaking as a thoughtful friend, not someone trying to convince a jury why Slocomb is a monster who should spend the rest of his life in prison."

"It's a tough call, isn't it?" Kevin said.

"So I've got three things to do tomorrow. The first is to have one more conversation with Slocomb. He's still Slocomb to me. I'm sure he'll keep his mouth shut, but I have to try to get him to tell me what happened to Eakins and Kennedy and why. Then I have to talk with Connie again, and do it in a way that is both honest and comforting, assuming that is possible. Unlike the Kennedys, where I tried to be helpful, I suspect that memorial services will be handled by Ernie's cycling buddies without my intervention. Finally, I have to get in touch with Prescott and begin the process of setting up a trial down in his jurisdiction. I'm sure he'll want to do it that way, but it's possible that there will be some political as well as legal hurdles. New York and Virginia don't always see eye to eye."

"Amazing, isn't it, that we still don't know, and maybe never will know, why Slocomb killed Eakins."

"I think we know. We talked about it, remember? Eakins visited Slocomb during the Gravel Grinder to get some water and saw or heard something that told him that a young African-American kid with down's syndrome was being mistreated by Slocomb. Eakins presumably threatened to report what he'd seen or heard, and Slocomb didn't dare let that happen. And Kennedy saw Eakins killed, which guaranteed that he'd be killed, too."

"None of which you can prove," Kevin said.

"Which is another reason why I'd like Prescott to get the credit for locking up Slocomb. Do you see my point?"

"I guess I do. But at least I know that you're the one that solved the case, not a southern sheriff."

"Let's not forget that without Sheriff Prescott I'd never have linked Slocomb to that racist rumble in Virginia. Anyway, if the trial down there lets him off with nothing more than a light sentence, I promise to have him back up here for another trial that I hope ends with life in the pen. And I don't mean the pig pen. I may want to spare Connie Eakins and the Kennedys from the worst of it, but I'm even more determined to put Slocomb away for a very long time. I've dealt with a few murderers, as you well know, but I've never met one I despise more than Slocomb. Sheer scum."

"You're telling me that the case isn't over. Right?"

"Cases like this are never over until the jury comes in. I'd rather it ends in a courthouse in Virginia, but I'm not issuing any case closed report. Not yet."

"Okay, I'll root for Prescott, but you're still my favorite sheriff. Come here - it's time for another kiss."

CPSIA information can be obtained
at www.ICGtesting.com
Printed in the USA
FFHW012133240319
47039217-56696FF